I swallow hard, and I don't take my eyes off of his.

I make my vows with an unwavering voice, and I'm not sure where that comes from. I'm not sure how I manage it. And then, the priest says that it's time for us to kiss. We've never done that.

He has touched my face, he has licked me between my legs, but he's never kissed my mouth.

And then, he leans in, and captures my lips. I am overcome. His mouth is a conqueror. Claiming me, my body, my mind. He thrusts his tongue deep into my mouth, and I capitulate him, allowing him entry. He wraps his arms around me, drawing me up against his large body, and I cling to him.

Lucian.

Enjoy this thrillingly dramatic royal trilogy by Millie Adams!

Young, Hot and Royal

Regal, reckless and in need of a ring!

You're cordially invited to the most outrageous royal wedding season of all!

Princess Emerald causes a scandal when she's kidnapped from the royal altar by her bodyguard... and father of her secret baby!

Enjoy the drama of *Princess, Pregnant, Prisoner*

Marrying merciless King Lucian might be the most dangerous decision of Lilith's life, until she realizes she's falling for her captor...

Get swept away by *King's Captive Bride*

Both available now!

Palace maid Birdie shares an incognito night with brooding King Onyx...only to discover she's secretly pregnant with the royal heir!

Don't miss Birdie and Onyx's story

Coming soon!

KING'S CAPTIVE BRIDE

MILLIE ADAMS

PRESENTS

If you purchased this book without a cover you should be aware that this book is stolen property. It was reported as "unsold and destroyed" to the publisher, and neither the author nor the publisher has received any payment for this "stripped book."

Recycling programs for this product may not exist in your area.

ISBN-13: 978-1-335-21383-9

King's Captive Bride

Copyright © 2026 by Millie Adams

All rights reserved. No part of this book may be used or reproduced in any manner whatsoever without written permission.

Without limiting the exclusive rights of any author, contributor or the publisher of this publication, any unauthorized use of this publication to train generative artificial intelligence (AI) technologies is expressly prohibited. Harlequin also exercises their rights under Article 4(3) of the Digital Single Market Directive 2019/790 and expressly reserves this publication from the text and data mining exception.

This is a work of fiction. Names, characters, places and incidents are either the product of the author's imagination or are used fictitiously. Any resemblance to actual persons, living or dead, businesses, companies, events or locales is entirely coincidental.

For questions and comments about the quality of this book, please contact us at CustomerService@Harlequin.com.

TM and ® are trademarks of Harlequin Enterprises ULC.

Harlequin Enterprises ULC
22 Adelaide St. West, 41st Floor
Toronto, Ontario M5H 4E3, Canada
www.Harlequin.com

HarperCollins Publishers
Macken House, 39/40 Mayor Street Upper,
Dublin 1, D01 C9W8, Ireland
www.HarperCollins.com

Printed in Lithuania

Millie Adams is the very dramatic pseudonym of *New York Times* bestselling author Maisey Yates. Happiest surrounded by yarn, her family and the small woodland creatures she calls pets, she lives in a small house on the edge of the woods, which allows her to escape in the way she loves best—in the pages of a book. She loves intense alpha heroes and the women who dare to go toe-to-toe with them.

Books by Millie Adams

Harlequin Presents

Her Impossible Boss's Baby
Italian's Christmas Acquisition
His Highness's Diamond Decree
After-Hours Heir
Dragos's Broken Vows
Promoted to Boss's Wife
Heir of Scandal
From Convent to Queen

The Diamond Club

Greek's Forbidden Temptation

Work Wives to Billionaires' Wives

Billionaire's Bride Bargain

Young, Hot and Royal

Princess, Pregnant, Prisoner

Visit the Author Profile page
at Harlequin.com for more titles.

CHAPTER ONE

A DRAGON'S HUNGER is only satiated by the blood of maidens.

I think about my grandmother's words now as my sister's cries of despair echo through the house.

"I can't marry him!" She's sobbing in earnest and I do feel bad for her, though I've always thought that level of emotion was an expense people in our position can't afford.

Eve is more fragile than I am. My mom has always said that—she isn't wrong. But my mom says it like it's a truth that can't be changed, and I'm not sure I agree with that. Eve knows she'll be taken care of—no matter what.

I'd love to be hard now. To leave her to the dragon. The Sea Serpent of the Mediterranean, our feared and reviled King Lucian.

The trouble is, I can't.

What lesson is she going to learn being wrenched away from the man she loves? I do believe she's in love with Marcus, even if I think love is a foolish endeavor. It's certainly never served any of the women in our family.

It's why my mother has two daughters with two men and neither of them are still here. Why my grandmother spent all her days living with us. Why her mother before her left England for Alabria—because she'd fallen in love with a man she'd met in London who told her to come here. She did. She had his baby. He abandoned her.

So we are three generations of women who have been abandoned by their husbands.

Love seems stupid to me.

I want more. I want to make a difference, to matter, to mean something. Love is fine; you can make a quiet life in a quiet house. I've already had that life. A life of struggle, a life where I am in the shadows of other people whether I want to be or not.

What I can't understand is being so distraught by an arranged marriage since no marriage has historically lasted till death in our bloodline.

Though with Lucian death could come sooner than expected…

On that she has cause for concern. That's the real worry that I have. The real fear that sticks in the pit of my stomach and makes me feel cold.

King Lucian has been married two times before. Both times to women from other countries. One princess, one duchess, and then he attempted a wedding last year to the Princess of Basilia, but she ran away with her bodyguard.

I suppose you could draw the conclusion that like us—he's cursed.

Or you could look at it the way I do. Which is that

since he's a man, and a whole king besides, his inability to hang onto a wife feels intentional, and is likely a character flaw.

In his case, perhaps that he's a killer.

That's the legend of the Sea Serpent of the Mediterranean. The dragon on the mountain. He is more myth than he is an actual man at this point, and his legend has expanded—some would say to hysterical proportions—through the years.

But he's done nothing to correct it.

There are rumors he's disfigured from the wars—which took place before I was born. There are rumors he was cursed by a witch and made half monster—I don't believe that. That's ridiculous.

Schoolchildren have rhymes about him. The mad king who might devour his subjects as soon as rule them.

He rules Alabria with an iron fist—he isn't a dictator by any stretch. But he controls the sky—not allowing planes to fly in or out. Every square inch of accessible coastline is patrolled heavily. No one gets in or out without him knowing. We're allowed in and out, but…

There was a war when he was born. Way before my time—he's forty years old to my twenty-two. I came along after the violence stopped. I don't know how it would have shaped me. My mom did what she does best during that time. She smoked and drank and had a nice time; she met men she liked and some she didn't. She worked—waiting tables or doing nails and hair for a while—she always took care of my grandmother and our modest house.

It's Eve's beauty that put her on his radar. He was determined—or so it was whispered—to marry a woman from Alabria this time. A woman to represent the people, from the people. His scouts looked far and wide for the right woman—and they happened upon Eve in the salon she works at.

"The Beautician and the Beast"—the headlines write themselves.

My family doesn't want headlines.

Mom has never really wanted to elevate herself, though the situation with money is a continual stress. If she didn't have to worry about bills, then things would be easier for her. If we don't do this, we may lose everything. If we do, my mother will never have to worry about money again.

Maybe then she wouldn't want for anything.

I suppose she would have liked to fall in love. I hope for her sake she still will.

She's cheerful about our lot in life, even as she struggles. Grandma wasn't cheerful so much as she was determined.

Eve is a dreamer.

I'm a planner.

I never planned to stay here. I've always wanted to leave. I wanted to go to Paris. To London. I wanted to see New York City. I've been saving and trying to arrange to get to university in another country. I have some money and I have a collection of scholarships and aid awards, and a few different options for school.

I'm older for a university student, but it's taken time for me to piece all of this together.

I want to be a scientist, a medical researcher. I want to matter far more than a peasant in a near-forgotten country. I want to change things. To make life better for other people.

The churn of humanity overwhelms and comforts me in equal measure. We are, by turns, expendable and infinitely precious all at once. But I had thought that if I could change something for the better…

It doesn't matter now.

In my mind I see a picture of my own closed fist. Holding onto everything I've ever wanted. Everything I was so close to having.

I imagine myself letting it go.

"I'll do it," I say.

I stand up from the dinner table, planting my hands firmly on the surface. Eve is still wailing and neither she nor my mom seem to have really heard what I said.

"I'll do it." The wailing stops. My mom looks at me. "I'll marry him instead."

"Lilith…" My mom looks like she pities me for a moment and I can't figure out why that would be.

"It isn't like he knows Eve. Why should he care?"

Eve exchanges a look with my mother. "He has seen me," she says. "In photos."

Oh. It's about Eve being prettier than me. They aren't wrong. She's redheaded with bouncy curls and vibrant green eyes. She looks a lot like his attempted-wife who ran away from him, actually. I saw her picture splashed all over the news afterward.

Eve is curvy and tall, and I've heard that King Lucian is six-five. I would look ridiculous with him. I'm plain. There's nothing wrong with that. I don't consider beauty a virtue, nor do I care overmuch about my looks.

I make myself as presentable as possible in every situation. But my blond hair is straight and fine and best served in a ponytail so it isn't just hanging lank around my face. My style is best described as: woman saving money to try to get to university out of the country.

Meaning: thrifted, and not in a trendy way.

I'm short. I'm petite with bony wrists, ankles and knees—I would never have really noticed that but Eve had a particular affinity for calling out the various prominent bones on my body when were children, to the degree where she once spent a summer calling me Knobby instead of Lilith—and I'm certainly not what you'd ever call a siren.

"I know I'm not as pretty as Eve," I say, because I'm nothing if not realistic about who I am.

Eve doesn't lord her beauty over me. She's always teased me the way a sister should. My mom and sister aren't trying to be mean in the veiled observation that I'm not the physical prize Eve would be. These are just facts.

But I'm not wounded. I know others might be, but I've never valued physical beauty.

"If he's just planning to kill you what does it matter if you're prettier than me?" I point this out, the ultimate pragmatism, I think.

"He didn't choose me for my brains or personality, Lil, which means he may have an opinion on you going in my place." She bites her bottom lip. "You're very pretty. But we don't look alike."

A testament to how much Eve and I have matured is that she isn't actually trying to tease me; she's framing it in practicality. She isn't wrong; even if we were equal in beauty we aren't the same, and men have types. I've heard.

Eve and I aren't the same type.

I realize that what Eve has just implied is that if he'd chosen her for her brains and personality, he *might* have taken me instead.

Which is a bit unfair to her. She's a lovely person. She's fun in a way *I've* never been, certainly.

"I know we don't, but honestly, his wives seem to come and go very quickly."

Eve starts to tear up again. "Lil, it's medieval!"

"I know," I say.

We don't have a choice. It was made very clear that he is expecting a bride—now. That Eve was not being asked, and it was heavily implied that a refusal would mean the whole family might spend the rest of their lives in prison.

It's hard to know if he would make good on the threat, though the legend of the man supports that, certainly.

One thing I also know is that if he is a killer, if he is a very, very awful man, I have a stronger chance of surviving than Eve. I'm not victim blaming, or saying the other women should have done something to protect themselves. I know my sister, though. She's soft. If it's too difficult she won't even want to live.

But I *do*.

I want to live and I want to do things. I want to make an impact. I could marry him, and maybe I could change things for the better. What if I could convince him to open up the skies? What if I could convince him to fund our university and fund more medical research?

What if I could take every change I wanted to make in myself, and bring it to Alabria?

Maybe I'm self-aggrandizing. My grandmother would probably say that.

She saw Eve and I as two sides to the same coin. Eve might want love and devotion and a much easier life, but Grandma saw it as no different than me dreaming of leaving. Of getting a job in scientific research.

I don't think they're the same at all. One of those things has very concrete steps. The other depends on men.

What I am aware of is that this will mean my dreams now depend on a man.

I don't love that.

But if Eve is forced into marriage with him then I won't be able to leave. I'll always be worried about her safety and well-being. I'll feel like I need to be close. Nothing will actually change.

In this scenario, she stays with our mother. She marries Marcus.

Our family will get money from the crown.

Mom won't have to work anymore. Eve will have her soft life.

"Eve, if you marry him it makes more problems than it solves. If I marry him it solves more than it makes."

She blinks. "Oh?"

"Yes. Trust me."

"The envoy is coming today!" Mom says. "You can't just bait and switch them."

"We'll see if I can. I'll try, anyway."

"You would do that for me?" Eve asks.

"Yes," I say.

"Why?" Her eyes are wide. "I'm your older sister. I should be protecting you."

But just like we all know Eve is prettier than I am, we know that she can't protect me. We know that I'm the one with the practical spirit. We know that it's me who would be the one we counted on if things got truly dire.

"You don't have to," I say.

"It seems like I should," she replies.

"There is no should. I want you to be happy. I really, really want you to be happy."

That much is true. I've never been searching for happiness, so much as purpose. And I can find purpose in this, something that I know Eve won't be able to do. She's never going to find purpose in suffering.

The truth is, I have no interest in marriage. I have no interest in romance. I don't even really have an interest in sex. I know about it. I know how to satisfy myself if need be. But I don't have strong fantasies of anyone or anything. It means that whatever the king wants, however he is, none of it matters to me.

Eve is like my mom. She loves the romance of it all.

The excitement. She loves when she meets a new man. And she has taken great joy in falling in love with Marcus. I don't think that it will last forever. Which isn't low confidence in my sister; it's just…her feelings are very intense. I don't think that necessarily makes him the best man on earth just because she thinks he is.

But she'll fall in love maybe ten times more, and enjoy it every single time. Being in the palace will stifle her. If it doesn't kill her.

"He's very old," she says, wrinkling her nose.

I laugh. "I don't care about that."

"You'll have to have children," she says.

I've never thought about that. Because along with not caring about men and dating goes my general lack of thought toward having a family of my own.

"I'll save that concern for later. None of his other wives have made it to the point where they could bear his children."

"I don't want you to die," Eve says, sniffling.

"I won't," I say. "I promise you that. Whatever happens, I will survive."

I rely on my mind to solve everything for me, and it is perhaps unrealistic of me to feel like my mind can save me here. Nothing suggests Lucian will be charmed by a brainy bride. But then…there is no real information and as far as I'm concerned, more information solves most things.

I also simply can't imagine allowing a man to have me killed. Again, not victim blaming, and I realize this might be unrealistic. But if my brain can't picture it, it's not real to me.

My brain paints a picture of my survival.

"I should go pack."

I stand up from the table, and I make my way up the stairs. I begin to pack briskly. I've thought about this before. What I would take with me if I were to leave. Because I've always planned on leaving.

There is a light knock on the door. "May I come in?"

I turn and see my mother standing there, her face lined with concern.

"Yes. Come in."

"It would kill her," she says softly.

I pause. "I know."

"You are clever. Cleverer than your sister." I feel guilty taking the compliment. I feel guilty agreeing.

"But you are cleverer than most people, Lilith. If I had my choice, I wouldn't send either of my daughters to that monster, but—"

"The crown didn't exactly make it optional," I say.

"No," she says.

"There is no use mourning over any of it," I say. "Just like there's no use being upset that we've always had to work so hard, that nothing has ever been easy. It simply is."

I'm practical.

Above all else, I'm practical.

"You will be safe. And if you…if you find yourself in danger, you should reach out to Princess Emerald."

Emerald. The woman who ran away from him at the altar.

"You think she could help me escape?" I ask.

"If anyone could. Or at the very least, help get your story out."

That was one of the things that I had always found interesting. There were no rumors that he had suppressed his wives' ability to communicate with the outside world. I find that troubling. Because in the event he is a murderer, then he must not signal his intent to kill them; it must just *happen.*

I'm going to need to look very closely for signals.

I pack, and I very deliberately do not take stock of the room. I don't turn it into something sentimental. I don't let myself get sad. And when the envoy arrives, I'm quick down the stairs. "My name is Lilith Carter," I say. "And I am taking my sister's place."

My escorts look at one another. I can see that they aren't sure quite what to do. "The king wants a wife." I refuse to look away from them. I refuse to be cowed in any way. "I volunteer for the position. You will not leave here empty-handed. However, if you try to take my sister…"

"One moment," the man says.

He steps back outside the house, and I hear muted voices. It sounds as if he made a phone call.

A moment later, he comes back in. "All right," he says. "You may come with us."

I clutch my bag more tightly in my hands. "All right," I agree. "Then let us go."

A dragon is only ever satisfied by the blood of maidens…

Well, I have the maiden part right. But I'm not sure that anything can ever satisfy this particular dragon.

Everything I've ever heard about him suggests that he is a black hole.

And a black hole can never be filled.

All it does is consume everything in its wake.

CHAPTER TWO

No one has seen King Lucian in years. I mean, that isn't strictly true. Many people have seen him. There were many people in attendance at the wedding that didn't happen last year. But there are never photographs at the events that he's at, and he never speaks on camera. He is seen, but only in the flesh, and in order to see him in the flesh you have to be someone of import.

My family has never been important.

Until we received word that the king had chosen my sister to be his wife.

Then, suddenly, we were important.

I don't feel important right now. I also don't feel especially practical. Suddenly, standing outside in the antechamber of the great iron palace that I have actually never seen in this close, and only ever seen in pictures online and from a great distance, I do not feel even a little bit brave.

Suddenly, I want to go back home and hide in my room.

All I've ever done is dream of leaving home. Plan for leaving home. I've never actually done it.

I'm more arrogant than I realized.

What I've done is work as a lab assistant and save money. That's it. Eve has at least dated. Fallen in love and out of love, tried different jobs, had her heart broken, broken hearts. She's lived more than I have and I convinced myself that because my goals were academic that somehow made me stronger.

I don't feel stronger now. I feel like what I am: a virgin who's never left home.

And who is about to be a dragon's breakfast.

Just because I've never valued certain kinds of knowledge doesn't mean I won't need it, and I'm overcome by that realization.

I try to conjure up the images I have seen of him.

They exist, but there's just not new media of him. At least nothing not taken from a very distant position. Anything new is grainy and indistinct.

Not that it matters how he looks. But I don't have a clear picture of him in my head as I both will the doors to the throne room to open, and try to will them to stay shut forever.

It doesn't matter what I want. The doors open both too late and too early.

I look up and I see him. The room might as well be kilometers long. He's all the way at the back, seated on a black throne, his shoulders straight, legs spread, hands on his knees. He's looking ahead, at me.

I realize he has no idea who I am or what I look like—not really. I know more about him than he does about me. Perhaps that puts me at an advantage in some way. At the very least, I'll cling to that like a lifeline.

"Approach."

I would have expected a command from him to sound distant, but no. It's like that word blooms inside my chest and spreads outward, filling me. Compelling me. All thoughts I had only a moment ago about claiming my advantage evaporate.

I can explain mitosis, but I can't explain anything that's happening in my body right now.

I feel frozen, and yet, my feet are moving. My body rushing to do his bidding. It feels like a crisis. How could it be anything else? One thing I'm not is biddable.

You're also not an idiot. Disobeying him right now could ruin everything.

Yes. I'm not being a doormat. I'm being smart. Within the realm of the very risky thing that I'm doing.

As I get closer to him, it feels as if the room gets larger, or perhaps I'm getting smaller. Like I'm shrinking beneath his uncompromising, icy gaze. By the time I get to the throne, I feel small enough to fit into someone's pocket.

And yet there is not a single pocket in the vicinity that I would trust.

"Give me your name."

He is an imposing figure. I knew he was scarred. Everyone knows that. What I didn't anticipate was how extreme the contrast is between that scarred flesh on his right side, and the pristine beauty of his left. His features are perfectly shaped. He has the strong features of a leader. A sharp nose, an expertly crafted jaw. If not for the scarring, he would be beautiful.

As it is, he's lethal. I've never seen anything like him.

The scars make his looks border on the demonic.

Because I can't look away from them, or him. Because he is handsome, somehow, and yet the word isn't quite strong enough.

I can tell, even with him sitting up on the raised throne, that he is as tall as rumored to be, if not more so. So far, he is all anyone has ever said.

And that is concerning.

I crane my neck, tilting my chin upward. "Lilith."

It is not, at the moment, his features that make him frightening. It's the fire in his eyes, which flares high and bright, and for a moment, I worry I'm in hell already. Like he might have dragged me down here with him, where everything is brimstone and intensity.

A black hole…

I look into his eyes, and they are fathomless.

There is no end to his depths. A black, bottomless well.

For the first time I'm properly afraid.

But I won't show it.

"Lilith and Eve," he said, thinking, considering. "An interesting combination of names. Did your mother do that intentionally?"

"Yes," I say. "And also no. By which I mean, she thought it was an amusing combination, and liked both names, but I don't think there is deep symbolism attached."

"Interesting. I was wondering if it meant that you were the disobedient one. After all, in mythology, she was the first wife of Adam, who was banished for not complying with his wishes."

"I am familiar," I say. "It is my name, after all."

"Well, it is good to know that you're familiar with your name. And why exactly do you think I should allow you to take your sister's place?"

"Because you don't actually care who your wife is." I'm taking a chance. I know it. I have no idea what King Lucian cares about. No one does. It's interesting that our first conversation is about myth. Because the man himself is more myth than reality. The idea that he might be a murderer is a popular one.

But there are also rumors that he's cursed. Destined to never find love because of a curse that a sorcerer put on his family before the start of the wars.

Standing there, looking at him, I think that perhaps he has never wanted love at all.

I have no idea what he wants.

"It's true," he says. "I decided to select a woman from Alabria. A commoner. I thought that it might perhaps boost morale among the people. To know that one of their own rules alongside me."

"Do you intend to have your wife rule alongside you?"

He tilts his head to the side, and he reminds me rather of a snake considering his prey. "I haven't decided yet. Tell me about yourself, Lilith."

It is a command. I can tell that he has never had a command directly disobeyed. I can also tell that this is a test.

Perhaps he's mad. Because I see these warring things in him. The fire in his eyes, the darkness too. He is a predator now, playing with his food, perhaps? Or is he just a jaded rich man looking to be entertained?

If so, why hide away?

He's a study in too many contradictions to make sense of him, which definitely suggests madness. And yet. For some reason I find him more compelling than repellent.

"I would like to know more about you," I say.

His lips curve, higher on the left than the right. "So you are disobedient. Interesting."

"Did you want compliance, Your Highness?"

"No," he says. "What I would like desperately is to not be bored."

This galvanizes me. I was right about him. He's bored. People often find me entertaining—even when I'm not trying to be funny. Whether it's because I'm forthright or just a bit bolder than a woman should be…

Though I don't feel bold. I just feel like me.

If it serves me here, though, then I'll use it.

And feel personally pleased that I was right about my ability to think my way out of it.

"Well, I'm not certain that I can help with entertainment. Are you sure you don't need a babysitter rather than a wife? Someone to arrange play dates?"

He is smiling fiercely now. "What I need," he says, "is a rehab of image. Whether I want one or not. The truth is, Alabria is becoming increasingly isolated from trading partners. And from the world itself. All of my attempts at marriages to fix this have failed, except for the union with Basilia. At least, the thwarted wedding resulted in a partnership."

"I imagine it's difficult to get other nations to partner with you when there's a possibility you've murdered the previous women that were sent to you."

I feel the guards near him take a step closer to me. He holds up a hand. "Bold of you to mention that."

"I don't see the point of not addressing the elephant in the room. Whether or not I…" I swallow hard. "Whether or not this marriage will be the end of me."

"I have no wish to harm you, little one. On that you can be certain."

To some, that might be an endearment. With him, it feels more cold observation.

It isn't actually an assurance that I will remain unharmed. Just that he doesn't wish to do it.

I recognize that I'm going to have to be content with that, however. At this point, anything he says is going to be suspect to me. I don't know him. I have no reason to trust him.

"Tell me about your sister," he says.

Trying a different tactic. I have, perhaps, earned some level of respect from him.

"She's lovely. Beautiful, I assume you knew that."

He nods. "I have a dossier about her. Your name is in it, but I confess that I know precious little about you. I did not ask for your information."

"If you have information about my sister then surely you know she's engaged to be married."

He considers this. "Yes."

"And yet, you were going to force her to marry you? You're doing a very good impersonation of the vile dictator that everybody thinks you are. If you want to rehabilitate your image, perhaps forcing a woman isn't the way to go about it."

He lifts a hand. "I am the king," he says.

As if it is a great honor. As if no one could possibly want anything other than to be in his presence, to be his wife. Not even to marry the man that they love. The man they are already engaged to.

"Not everyone wants power."

He leans forward. "You do."

The words are soft, and yet they reverberate through me as a threat. A threat of recognition. Like he sees something inside of me that maybe I've never seen in myself. It scares me. Because it feels true, but I would say that it's not. I don't care about power. I care about education. I care about discovery. I care about being able to change my position in life, and change things for other people. Though, I suppose what is wanting control over your life but the pursuit of power?

I would have said it was just a quest for agency.

Funnily enough, I'm standing here offering to trade a substantial amount of mine away.

And yet, it is a choice that I made.

"What I want is for my sister to be able to marry the man she loves."

"A martyr. How delightful. I've heard the blood of martyrs is particularly invigorating."

"You'll only find out if you marry me," I say.

"I could always go back to the drawing board. Find a different family. A different woman."

That he's open to finding someone new, without threats, makes me feel slightly dizzy.

"You could," I say.

I hold my breath for a beat. Perhaps I'm about to get my freedom.

Then I see that fire in his eyes again.

"I don't think I will, though." He snaps his fingers, and the guards move forward. "Take Lilith to her new quarters in the north tower."

"I'm not a prisoner," I say.

"No," he says. "But you're not free either."

This, likely, comes from his previous bride fleeing the wedding.

His words send a shock through my body. And suddenly I'm flanked by guards. "I can go on my own."

"No," he says. Then he tilts his head again. I can't quite figure out what it means when he does that. He's assessing something. Evaluating it. Me.

Then he stands, and begins to walk down the steps of the throne. His cape billows behind him as he approaches me, and if I felt small before, I have never felt more insubstantial than I do right now.

I know a lot about the physiology of the human body. Necessary for medical research. But I can't explain the way that the air seems to exit my lungs in a gust, uncontrolled, and without my bidding.

"I will walk with you."

I have to tilt my head upward to actually look at his face. "I don't think that's necessary."

"I'm going to be your husband," he says. "You shouldn't be afraid of me."

I feel as if ropes are tightening around my body. I'm trapped now and it's official. I am going to be his bride.

I've succeeded.

In ending my life as I know it.

"I think in your case a lack of fear will have to be earned," I say, craning my neck upward and looking at him as directly as I can.

Those ice-colored eyes glitter. "I don't think you're afraid of very much."

"No."

He steps down off the last step, and walks around me in a slow circle, like he's evaluating a horse. "You're very small," he says. "You remind me of a sparrow. The way you move your head, looking like you want to hop off. Or perhaps fly away."

I don't like the characterization. My sister would have been some glorious tropical bird. Of course I'm a sparrow. Small and plain. I don't know why it bothers me. It shouldn't.

"And you're a dragon," I say. Because for all that I am intimidated, for all that I feel unequal to this moment, shamed by it, even, I have pride.

Had he been a dragon in truth, I would've seen smoke curl out of his nostrils then. He smiles, the slow satisfaction spreading on his face filling me with a strange sort of terror.

There is something villainous about that smile. It isn't a show of happiness or warmth.

"Come with me, sparrow."

He begins to walk away from me, leaving me to run to catch up with him. "You can't walk that quickly," I say, my legs working as quickly as they can. "You're too much taller than me."

"You seem to be keeping up just fine."

I am overcome by a sense of surreality. This can't be happening. I cannot be chasing after the king of my country, on the verge of becoming his wife.

His wife.

I am not meant to be someone's wife. I'm going to be a scientist.

Except no. I'm going to be a queen.

There are so many girls who dream of things like this. Of finding out that they're royalty. That they were always destined to be. Not me.

But I think again of poor Eve, and how much she wants to marry Marcus. And I think maybe I'm actually wrong. I'm not sure that most women dream of marrying strangers. I think they dream of being safe and happy, of knowing that their problems will be taken care of, and sometimes that fantasy takes the shape of becoming a princess. But when given the choice between royalty and love, Eve chose love.

And I chose love too. The love of my sister.

I chose it over my own dreams.

Not for the first time, I wonder if I've made a terrible mistake.

We exit the throne room, and cross a great antechamber, heading to a spiral staircase, tight and narrow, that winds up and up and up.

"Are the stairs the only way of getting there?"

"Yes," he says.

"And my room is up there?"

"As is mine," he says.

"Oh." There's no way that we are going to share a room. Royalty doesn't do that. And I don't know him.

"You have a separate room," I say.

He chuckles. "Yes. Of course. As is fitting."

I feel mollified by this.

But my thighs are burning, and the backs of my calves are weeping for relief. There must be five hundred stairs. And I'm dizzy from the tight spiral.

"This is medieval."

"You are such a small thing. I would think carrying yourself up the stairs would be easy."

"I'm more of a…reader. Than a person who climbs."

"I see. And what do you like to read?"

"Science textbooks."

He makes a noise in the back of his throat. It sounds disappointed.

"I don't like nonfiction very much. I prefer the classics. Romantic literature."

"You do?"

"Yes," he says. "Why is that a surprise?"

"Because. You're…"

"I'm kidding," he says. "I know exactly why it's a surprise. But don't believe everything that you've heard about me, sparrow. Most of it isn't true."

"Why would people lie about you?"

"They aren't lying on purpose. I'm like God, in many ways. People invent stories about me to feel closer to me, to demystify me. To know me. But they don't know me. No one does."

"No one?"

"No one," he repeats.

And just then, we reach the top of the stairs. "Our rooms are the only rooms here."

"Does your poor staff have to climb all those stairs to bring things to you?"

He laughed. "There is a service elevator. I lied to you."

"You… You…"

"Come," he says, taking me down the short hallway, and to an ornate gold door.

There is a tree embossed on the door, apples hanging from the branches. Beneath it is a serpent, and a woman.

"Well, that is a bit on the nose," I say.

"You see, when I found your sister I thought it was amusing. I think this is better."

I don't ask why. Instead, I wrap my hand around the doorknob and push the door open. The room inside is beyond opulent. It's like nothing I've ever seen before. It is itself a whole fairy tale. The bed is gold, like the door, the four posters fashioned to be like tree branches. Winding and spiraling up toward the ceiling, and then arcing toward one another to meet and twine around each other in the middle. There is soft pink fabric draped over the gold. The blankets and pillows on the bed are sumptuous and lovely.

I have never even fantasized about luxury on this level. I dreamed of other things.

But I can't deny that this is…

"Is it to your liking?"

"What's not to like?"

"You like science, and I wasn't expecting you. Had

I known perhaps I would have made a room more to your taste."

"Does me liking science mean I can't also like pretty things?"

"Yes," he says.

I laugh at him. I can't help it. "That's a ridiculous thing to say. Science is beautiful. My study focus is going to be biology. The study of life. Of the building blocks that make up everything around us. What's more beautiful than that?"

I realize then that I have made assumptions. Because I spoke about my studies like they might still be possible. I don't know if that's true. I don't know anything.

My life is no longer guaranteed, in any capacity.

"Interesting," he says. "I suppose I've never seen it that way. It was simply a subject that used to put me to sleep in school. I would much rather read. The images that words paint are sometimes the only things strong enough to blot out ugly memories."

It's a profound statement. And one that makes me curious, but I can see that I've lost him.

"I believe you," he says. "When you need food, simply pick up the phone and order. And it will be brought to you. Using the service elevator."

"Can I use the service elevator?" I ask.

"You are going to be queen, sparrow. You can do whatever you like."

But much in the same way that I am not a prisoner, but not quite free, I know that I cannot actually do whatever I like. It's only that I do not know exactly what is forbidden to me.

He leaves, closing the door firmly behind him, and I am struck by the scene on that side of the door. A naked man and woman, standing together. It's not the same woman with the snake.

I move closer, and begin to extend my hand, and then I drop it.

I shake my head.

Then I walk over to the bed and sit down. I replay the last hour in my mind. My hands begin to shake uncontrollably, and I look down at them, trying to regain control.

I can't.

Then I burst into tears.

CHAPTER THREE

I CRY UNTIL I fall asleep. The burst of emotion is unexpected. I've been powering through everything, every hardship, every thwarted and delayed dream for so many years, and it's as if I've finally hit a breaking point.

I see his blue eyes in my mind. His great and terrible beauty.

He himself is a breaking point.

When I wake up, I look out the window and see stars. I rub my eyes, and my stomach growls. I'm sure that I've missed my window to get food.

I sit up in bed, and then, before I even realize what I'm reacting to, I startle and begin to prepare myself to run.

Because there's someone in the corner of my room. Sitting.

And then my brain catches up and I realize it must be him.

The king.

He is in the same posture that he sat in when I first arrived in the throne room. Hands planted on his knees, legs spread wide. I can feel him looking at me. I already know, even with his face obscured in shadow, that he is tilting his head, evaluating me in that way of his.

I am fully clothed, but I pull the covers up higher as if they might protect me from his gaze. That he's been sitting there watching me sleep makes me feel exposed, and I don't like it.

"What are you doing in my room?"

"I asked in the kitchen if you had ordered dinner. They said no. I began to worry that you had thrown yourself out the window."

"Well, you did say there was a service elevator. I'm much more likely to take that than I am to fling myself to the rocks below."

He shrugs. "You would be surprised."

His words send a chill down my spine. "Well, I'm fine. I just fell asleep."

"You must be hungry."

"I'm not," I say. But my stomach growls, calling me a liar. I can tell by the way he shifts that he's heard it.

He leans forward, a shaft of moonlight falling over his face. "Don't be foolish. You will come downstairs and eat."

"I will not," I say. Refusing him just to establish some form of independence.

"Enough," he says.

He stands and makes his way over to the bed, holding his hand out to me. "Do not engage in foolishness with me, sparrow."

"My name is Lilith."

"I know," he says. "But you are Lilith to everyone. To me, you are sparrow." I look at his extended hand.

Ignore it, and I get out of bed. My body feels heavy. So does my soul.

“There is no need to be difficult,” he says, his words a sharp reproach. “Remember, I did not force you to come here.”

“No. You were only going to force my sister.”

He makes a noise that I assume is agreement.

“I did,” he says. “But it has all worked out in the end.”

I grind my back teeth together, deciding that there is no point in continuing to fight with him. I gave in to despair earlier, and I won’t do that again. My lifetime of careful planning has crumbled. I made an impulsive decision. Something I’ve never done before in my life. And now I’m dealing with the consequences.

“Why are we taking the stairs?” I complain as I realize he’s leading us back down that tight, steep spiral.

“I prefer it,” he says.

“And is everything about your preference?”

“Yes.”

I ponder this. He’s the king, so I suppose that’s true. Nothing has ever been about my preference. I can’t even access that. The level of selfishness.

“I guess that’s what it’s like when you have endless resources so no one ever has to compromise or share.”

“I also have no family,” he says. “Tell me about yours.”

“Surely you’ve read about my family in whatever dossier you received about Eve.”

“And you’ve heard about me. The great and terrible

Sea Serpent of the Mediterranean, yet you don't know me. Speak to me, sparrow."

He breezes past that remark so quickly that I can't get a foothold in it. Can't read his emotion.

If there is any at all.

"It's my mother, myself and Eve. For most of my life, we also lived with my grandmother. But she..." My words catch in my throat. "She died. Three years ago."

"I see. People have a distressing habit of doing that. Dying."

"Well, yes. It's sort of the way things work."

"True."

"My mom is a hairdresser. My sister... She does nails right now. Though, she's the kind of person who gets bored very quickly with certain things, so I imagine that she'll learn a new skill, and quickly figure out a way to make money doing that. She used to bake. Before that she did little miniature paintings of people's pets."

"Well, that sounds extremely enterprising."

"It is," I say.

"But you like science."

"Yes."

"An odd sparrow in the nest."

I think of my mother and my sister. Both so pretty and colorful.

"Yes," I say. It's honest, anyway. I'm not sure that he deserves my honesty, but there's also no point in me not admitting it.

"But you love your sister so much that you took her

place? Or do you secretly yearn to be the one in the spotlight?"

The question feels like a spotlight. And he makes me question myself. I do yearn to be someone who makes an impact. Does that mean I crave attention more than I realize? I don't want to be insignificant. I know that much.

But there is much to do first before I earn any sort of attention.

"I don't yearn for the spotlight," I say. "I…yearn for university."

"To study biology."

"Well. Yes. Medical research, that's what I ultimately want to do."

"Interesting. I will take that under advisement."

Finally, we exit the endless spiral staircase, and are back in the big empty antechamber. I follow him to another corridor, and down a long hallway all the way to the end until we arrive at a large dining room with a table that could easily seat a hundred people.

He gestures to his seat at the end. "Take your seat. I will ensure that your food is brought directly."

I think about arguing, but I don't, partly because my legs hurt after running the stair gauntlet again. He vanishes for a moment, then reappears, taking his spot at the head of the table. I realize that I am at his right hand. I can't tell if that's significant or not. I'm having a difficult time figuring him out at all.

If he's a madman, then there is no figuring him out.

That is something that must be taken into consideration.

But I certainly didn't expect for him to be trying to spend any time with me. I figured that I would appear, and he would either wave a hand and send me to the dungeon, or he would kill me. He's done neither, and I don't know what to do with that as a development.

Now he's sitting there, staring at me like I'm a puzzle that he wants to solve.

I'm probably looking at him in much the same way.

Only a moment later, a heaping plate of food is brought in. There is roasted chicken and beef. Mashed potatoes, vegetables. I haven't seen a meal like that… maybe ever. My mom isn't much of a cook. Well, none of us are. We take turns, because that's only fair.

But that means that our meals are cheap and simple. This is nothing like that.

And there's so much butter. On everything. I try to hide my delight, because I don't want him to know that this is one of the more exciting things to ever happen to me. Obviously, I fail at that, because when I take a bite of the mashed potatoes, something appears in his eyes, and he leans in. "You like that?"

"Yes," I say. "What's not to like? Obviously your chef is very good."

"What is your favorite thing to eat?"

"I…" I don't want to tell him that I don't know. But the truth is, I am right at this moment eating the best thing that I've ever had in my entire life, and I would not have said that mashed potatoes were my favorite food. But these mashed potatoes are.

"I don't know," I say finally.

"You don't know?" He's looking at me like that

again. That keen, serpentlike examining. "We shall have to find out what it is."

"Shall we?" I bite back the question as to whether or not it's so he knows what to make for my last meal.

I probably shouldn't bring death up every time I'm with him. If it's on his to-do list and it slipped his mind for a moment, I shouldn't remind him.

I take another bite of the food, and I am tempted to tell him that right now, whatever all this is, is the very best thing I have ever eaten. I don't. I feel that it is a bit much to act grateful.

"What sorts of things do you wish to do as queen?"

The subject changes abruptly, and I have to chew and swallow my food before I can answer. "Well, as I've mentioned, I wish to study."

"Yes. But as queen, the scope of your duties will encompass overseeing certain programs for the nation."

"Well. I've lived among your people for all of my life. So I have a lot of opinions about the way the country is run."

"Do you?" he asks. "Excellent. Tell me."

"Do you really want me to…point out the flaws in your present system?"

"Yes," he says. "This is all about improving things for our people."

I'm surprised by this. But then, I've been completely surprised by him from the moment I first met him. There are ways in which he's just like the stories. But also…he isn't.

The myth of King Lucian is just that. A myth.

Though, I'm not entirely sure if the version that is

sitting in front of me right now is better than those myths or worse. I can't tell if I'm being played with. Like a mouse rather than a sparrow. Or if he's being somewhat sincere.

"I would really like to see increased funding for education. The public school system as well as the universities here. The public universities in Alabria lag behind the rest of the world. I was going to go to university in England. Most likely. I was looking at a few places around the world, but the idea of going here was never one I took seriously. The investment in research simply isn't there."

"Then we will invest in research," he says.

"You… Just like that?"

"You have the ear of the crown, sparrow."

"And will I be able to study?"

"Perhaps in a fashion. We will see. There is the matter of heirs."

My stomach clenches tight. "Yes. I am aware of that… But surely we can delay. I'm only twenty-two."

He makes a regretful sound in the back of his throat. "So young."

"You could have chosen someone older. My sister is only twenty-four."

"Alas, it is impractical when one must see to the production of heirs."

"That feels a bit unfair." It is a function of science, and I know well that science doesn't care about feelings. Even so.

"It is," he says. "Life is often unfair."

I know that, and I'm not generally bothered by it.

I've worked to make my life the best that I can in spite of the modest circumstances I was born into. I'm well aware that life isn't fair. That we aren't all given the same tools, the same resources, the same starting point.

Hearing it from a king—the man who owns this palace, and who now owns me—is grating.

"I've noticed," I say. "Especially when some have all the money and power and others have to scrape the crumbs of it from the floor."

"Is this how you feel about your own life?"

"It's how so many people feel about their own lives."

"Are you anti-monarchy?" he asks, studying me intently.

"I'm too practical for that. The abolition of government is unlikely as long as men want power—and spoiler, I don't think men will ever not want power. A monarchy is just one of the many imperfect and corruptible styles of government. You rid yourself of one, you only get another. Ask the Romanovs."

"A philosopher, then, if not an anti-monarchist."

I blink. "I don't think so. I'm only practical."

"Only practical?" he asks. "Is that all you are, little sparrow?"

I think about my life. All the years I've spent studying and working hard to get where I wanted to go. Then how I demolished it all when my sister wept.

"No," I say. "I'm not only practical."

Sacrificing myself for my sister wasn't practical.

He moves nearer to me and my breath catches. Then there are footsteps at the threshold of the room, servants appear and clear our plates, and he has not moved away from me, but he doesn't move forward anymore.

He is frozen and my breath is caught in my chest as my heart tries to burrow its way straight through the front of my chest cavity.

New plates are placed before us, with decadent-looking cakes on them. My mouth waters in spite of myself. I look up at him and my heart begins to race.

No, I'm not always practical. This isn't practical at all.

I take a bit of my cake, and he doesn't move toward his. He's watching me. He keeps his eyes trained on me the whole time. In defiance of that, I don't stop what I'm doing. I eat every last bite without asking what his problem is or why he's watching me. I won't give him the satisfaction of knowing I find him perplexing.

As soon as I take that last bite he moves. He leans in and presses his thumb against the corner of my mouth and wipes away a bit of frosting. Then, without looking away, he draws back and brings his thumb to his lips, licking the traces of sweetness away.

My stomach hollows out and drops into my feet.

"You know," he says. "I am not a fan of overly sweet things. But this may have changed my mind."

My brain synapses are firing, sparking, trying to come to some conclusion about what he's just said. Trying to make it about something other than…sex.

I have no experience with men or sex. Really none at all with attraction that exists outside the secret places in my mind. Fantasy is one thing, but to have a real man looking at me like this, so close, so in control of me, so dangerous to me, is beyond the scope of my ability to fathom.

I say nothing, and then he takes hold of my chin, his thumb and forefinger squeezing tight. “I might be King of Alabria. But I am also your king, sparrow.”

“Isn’t that the same thing?” I ask, my voice trembling.

He releases his hold on me and I feel the impact of his ice-cold eyes all the way down to my toes. “No.”

Then he stands, his impossible height dwarfing me as I sit still, my empty cake plate in front of me.

“Can you find your way back to your room?”

“Yes.”

“Good. I will see tomorrow.”

He gives no indication of what tomorrow will bring.

CHAPTER FOUR

The Dragon

HUNGER IS NOTHING new for me. Hunger is a way of life. I have all the money and power in the world, and yet a keen sense of what I cannot buy. What I can't force, what I can't hold onto. There are certain things the universe will tear from your cold, bleeding hands as you weep and beg. There is no compassion out there among the stars.

When you come into possession of something all you can do is hold as tightly to it as possible, imprison it if you must. Whatever you can do to hang on as long as you can.

A sparrow cannot fly if you clip its wings.

CHAPTER FIVE

When I wake up I'm pulled out of bed almost immediately by one of the palace aides, and dragged into a massive room with racks of clothing and a hairstyling station.

I'm no stranger to having my hair colored, cut and otherwise experimented on. After all, my mom and sister often had to have a guinea pig for new techniques they were trying to learn. But I find that I'm anxious about turning my hair over to someone I've never met.

Yet, it's only hair, and on the long and vast list of concerns I have right now, my hair shouldn't be one of them.

I can't figure out my future husband. I have no idea what he intends to do with me, or what my life will look like once he assumes control of it.

Once he does? He already has.

I let that truth sit and turn over in my stomach. I don't like it, but I can't deny it.

"The king has tasked us with overseeing your look for the wedding celebration in the coming days."

"Oh," I say. I have no idea what the wedding celebration is. If it's the wedding itself, I actually don't even know when we are supposed to be getting married. It's tempting to sit there, asking no questions. Because I'm not entirely sure that I want the answers. But if there's anything I've learned from science it's that inquiry is the only way to learn. Trying, failing, finding answers you don't like is all a part of reality.

And the truth doesn't change just because you don't know it. Facts truly don't care about your feelings. And so if I want facts I can't afford to care overmuch about my feelings either.

"And what exactly is the wedding celebration?"

The woman looks at me just as I feared she would. She's a very beautiful woman, and probably feels that she's more sophisticated than I am. Certainly prettier. She would be correct. I wonder if she thinks that she would be a better candidate for queen than I am. All of that is probably true. But still, I don't like being the object of somebody's petty jealousy when I don't even especially want to be in the position that I'm in. But then, perversely, that makes me want to lean into my ignorance here. Because it will only make her think that I'm all the more unsuitable, and that will likely make her angry.

"There will be a party the day before the wedding. A time for all of the foreign dignitaries to come and celebrate your upcoming union."

"When would that be?"

She stares at me. "You don't know?"

"Yes. Our great and glorious king likes to keep me in suspense about everything. But most of all my fate."

I can tell that she's shocked that I would say something so dry about the man himself. But surely everybody who deals with him on a daily basis can see what a mercurial and difficult person he is.

Even if he isn't a murderer, and I'm still withholding judgment on that, he doesn't do anything to make his movements clear. To make his intentions transparent. If anything, he seems to delight in his own opacity.

"The wedding will be Sunday," she says.

"I see. You must know then, that there was another bride intended for this wedding originally."

She nods. "Yes. I was given an entirely different color profile, and I had to change everything. Also, your measurements are different."

I laughed. "Oh, I know. The original bride was my sister."

I can tell that she's curious. Her curiosity is warring with her irritation at my existence. "My sister is in love with someone else," I say. "I stepped in because I'm not in love with anyone."

"And you get to be the queen."

"I didn't want to be queen either."

This gags her. I'm amused. I can't tell if she likes me less or more after the admission. But she proceeds to show me clothing on a rack, dresses of so many different colors, and I confess that I have no idea what color suits me the most. I've never thought about it.

"You've never thought about what color looks best on you?" She is incredulous.

"Yes. At no point in my life has that mattered. It has never gotten me anything. My sister is a great beauty. And in order for beauty to provide you with some sort of privilege or upward mobility, it must be a great and terrible beauty indeed. You possess beauty like that," I say to her.

That makes her almost angry. "And yet, you are to be queen, and I am a stylist."

"Are you in love with him?"

She laughs. "Oh. No. He's terrifying."

"Yes," I agree. "What's your name?"

She frowns. "Allison."

"Well, Allison, if you would like to ask the king if he would approve of the two of us switching places, I really don't mind."

I'm sort of kidding. Except, after the words exit my mouth I realize I'm not. Maybe I can keep switching queens in and out, and eventually we'll find someone who actually wants the position. Not someone who is simply doing it because they were commanded to, or to help someone else.

"I…"

"Oh, you don't actually want to marry him."

"He's…beautiful. And powerful, rich. Those are all interesting things, I grant you. But…"

"Less envious at the idea of me marrying him when you have to actually imagine what that would look like."

"I don't know," she says. "I didn't realize that my attitude was so apparent. I apologize. It's an interesting fantasy. The idea that your whole life could change overnight because the king wants to marry one of his common citizens. But I guess it's only good in theory."

"I'm hoping that it won't be horrible in practice. But I won't know until after."

"Are you afraid of him?"

I think about it. About everything I've seen of him since I've arrived. "I think anyone would be foolish to not be afraid of him in some capacity. He's an extremely intimidating man."

"Men like him are either fantastic in bed, or terrible." She laughs. "There's no in between. He is horrendously arrogant, but also, he has those scars. He has that sort of rough, distorted beauty, which sometimes gives a man a bit of humility, but doesn't make him any less good in the sheets."

I stare at her like everything she's said is in a foreign language. To me, it might as well be. Because I don't understand any of that. Not really.

Liar. You don't want to.

"I confess to you that is the least of my concern."

"Well, it's not a small concern," she says. "Though I assume he's proportional."

I am caught on that statement while different dresses are taken off of me and put back on, as I am twirled and twisted in front of a mirror.

"Your eyes are very nearly green," she says. "Blue and green clothes seem to bring that out."

I stare at myself, wrapped in blue silk currently. I do see something a bit mossy in my eyes, versus the typical indistinct mud I would normally claim to have. It's also surprising to me how nicely the dress highlights what little I have in terms of curves. Again, nothing

I've spent much time thinking about, but the reality is, someone is now going to see them.

Not just someone. Him.

Do I want him to be good in bed? That is actually the key question. Not whether or not he is. But do I want to derive any pleasure from the union at all?

My disinterest in the topic won't help me. Because he's intent on having children with me.

"Are you all right?" Allison asks me.

"I have been significantly better," I respond.

"Should I choose the dress for you?"

While I end up adding several pieces in green and blue to my wardrobe, the dress that she chooses for the night of the wedding party is gold. It makes my skin look warm, my hair look more like honey, rather than a dull dishwater sort of color. And after that, I sit down with the stylist, who enhances all that gold, and eliminates the dishwater altogether.

I receive facial treatments that make me glow, and when I try everything on at the end, complete with makeup—left subtle at my request—I hardly recognize the woman in the mirror.

"Beauty," Allison says, looking at me, "is often a reflection of effort. And money."

"I was too poor to be beautiful before," I quip.

"You were always beautiful," she says. We're friends now; I'm not quite sure how that happened. "This just makes it clear to everyone, before you had the kind of beauty that someone has to look for. I don't mean that as a backhanded compliment. I just mean that people are always looking for something flashy. And that definitely wasn't you. But it can be. You're shimmering now."

I'm completely uncomfortable with both the statement and with my appearance. And when she dresses me in a pair of extremely expensive jeans, and a white cashmere sweater, a simple gold bracelet and a necklace with a single string of diamonds all the way around, I am discomfited by how much I like what I see. Because it looks so simple, effortless. And yet I know how much effort went into it. Even the ponytail my hair is styled in is artful in a way that I'm not sure I could ever replicate.

Except, I don't have to, because I can have my hair done every day if I want to. But I still can't go to university. That's an extremely strange realization.

"The king wishes to see you in your quarters."

I turn and face the king's aide, who is standing in the doorway, unable to hide the shock on his face when he sees me. Okay. I do look much improved.

It's so strange to feel a small amount of pleasure in that, when I never cared before.

"All right," I say, and I allow him to lead me from the room. I say goodbye to Allison, who I know I will see again, because I have no intention of ever choosing clothing again without her expertise.

A strange feeling of worry begins to chew its way through my stomach. Is this going to change me?

There's already so much for me to grapple with that adding that to my list of concerns is something I really don't want to do.

"We can take the elevator," he says.

I laugh, but I don't tell him why. Of course, Lucian seems opposed to the elevator.

Or at least, he doesn't want me to be able to use it.

He's such a strange man.

That's a funny thought. But he is strange. He doesn't behave like any other human being I've ever met. He also doesn't behave quite like the monster I expected him to be. He is a creature entirely apart from any behavior I've ever witnessed before.

He is beautiful. Allison is right about that. It's almost otherworldly, though. And yet, he touched me last night.

The response it created in my body was wholly foreign to me. I've experienced desire before, yes, or rather I would say I've experienced arousal. In the most basic, physiological sense. Always and only theoretical, and in the confines of fantasies that I am utterly in control of.

Men, I can solve like a puzzle. Men who make sense, like science.

Lucian is not like that.

When he put his hand on me I was so aware of how little control I have with him. The idea sends a shiver of dread down my spine. I tell myself that it's dread. Because if it's something else than…

No. I refuse to think about it.

I refuse.

We arrive at my room shortly, and I push the door open. Lucian is inside, as if it is his room, and not mine. He has absolutely no respect for boundaries. But then, I suppose everything in the palace is his. Everything in the country is his. I wonder if he feels like anything is forbidden to him, or if he feels like all of this is his due. If he feels like everything and everyone is simply renting a piece of this place that belongs to him, and he is the rightful owner of it all.

Simply because he was born to the throne.

He has been the king for as long as I've been alive.

The gap in our ages feels so vast at the moment. Along with the gap in our power, wealth and authority.

He has lived a whole life additional to mine. And also, wields so much more control than I ever will.

He turns to face me, and something ignites in his ice-blue eyes. The response that he has to my makeover is different than the response the aide had. It's nothing like simple recognition. I am immobilized by the expression on his face. There is something so intense there, so dark. Like he is exercising an intense amount of control to continue to just keep standing there. To not move on me. Devour me.

He looks hungry. He looks like a predator. I cannot tell whether I want to run away from him, or whether I want to stand and see what he'll do. Whether I'm frightened or fascinated.

It's the same feeling that I had last night, only amplified. When he touched my chin I felt things in my body that I have never felt before.

And the truth of the situation simply didn't matter.

Not that he might be a murderer. Not that I'm being forced into all of this. Not that I should be outraged, and never, ever attracted to him.

There is so much to fear. The fact that he now has

total and complete dominion over my life. The fact that I am to be a royal broodmare. The fact that when I marry him he is going to have husbandly rights to my body, and as the king…

Does he feel he owns me as well?

"I see that you have been with the royal stylist today."

"Yes," I say. I watch him closely, because as small and undone as I feel in this moment, I recognize that he also feels something. His feelings might be the key to my power.

If I can learn to wield them. If I can learn to find real meaning in them.

The sound he makes, a deep growl in the back of his throat, speaks of approval, though I can't say how I know that. Only that I feel it. In the way that he looks at me. In the way that my body feels as his eyes skim over me.

"You look…" He moves nearer to me, and then he begins to circle me, slowly. My heart starts to beat faster. I can't breathe. It's so difficult for me to think. I always think. My mind is the one thing that I can count on. It's the thing I've been counting on for a very long time, to get me out of trouble, to change my life. And I can't use it right now. There is nothing except for the insistent throbbing of my heart, and the trembling in my body. "Expensive," he says finally. "You look expensive."

I don't know what to make of that comment. I'm not sure if I should be insulted by it or complimented. I'm not sure if I should ever be complimented by him.

I did choose this. But just because I'm a willing prisoner doesn't mean I'm less of a prisoner. My options are limited.

"Thank you," I say. "But if I look expensive it's only because it was purchased with your money."

"A better use of it I could not think of." He looks around my bedroom, and for the first time, I realize why he's called me up here. I was blinded by his presence. But now I see…bookshelves. Floor to ceiling, and entirely full. "Except for this."

"What is this?" I ask, feeling breathless.

"It is for you," he says. "Your own private library. Obviously, there is room for it to expand, I didn't want to make all of the choices for you, but I wanted it to be robust when you saw it at first. Every title in here is on a scientific subject. Except the shelf," he says, gesturing to one next to the bed. "Those are novels, ones that I think you should read. In spite of the fact that you claim to dislike fiction."

"You think that you can change my mind?"

"I'm quite certain that if you don't like fiction it's because you haven't read the right books."

There is something in the confidence of that statement that makes my stomach go tight. There is something in that certainty that I know will apply to other things. And I might not fully understand all of these things, the way that things are between men and women. The way that things will be between the two of us. And yet, I feel this as an echo of that.

And yet, he's also given me shelves and shelves full of the books I do want.

He cares about what I want.

The realization shocks me.

"You did all this for me?"

"Of course," he says. "I want you to like it here. I want you to be comfortable."

"You…you want me to like this?"

"Of course I do," he says, as if it is the most ridiculous thing he's ever heard, the idea that this man who makes edicts out of other people's lives might not care about their happiness. "Your time will be spent here, in the majority—you must have access to the things that bring you joy."

I am rattled by this. By this statement that I'm going to spend most of my time here.

"What about the potential for studying at university?"

"We have the ability to bring top-tier teachers in for you. For you to join in classes virtually anywhere in the world. There is no need for you to go to university."

"But…" I realize that it was a childish thought. I realize of course that there is no queen or king sitting in a classroom in a regular university, living in another country. That there's no way he would ever let me live away from him, especially not because he sees me as his potential baby factory. But hearing the words, fully having to accept it…

Perhaps I wanted a different life more than I realized.

More than education, but a chance to be away from here.

I then realize how much I was hoping he would simply change his mind. How much I was hoping that he would realize that I was young and I deserved to do more. How much I was hoping that this would all magically work out. I thought that I was practical.

I'm not.

I'm just a girl. One full of hope that I have no right to have.

One full of an unrealistic and shattering amount of optimism. I've walked myself into a prison, and I was so certain that because I had done it of my own accord, that I would have some control over when the door was locked.

But this man is my jailer. And what he says is what will be.

I had too much confidence in myself.

"I was hoping that I might actually go somewhere for school," I say.

"It is impossible," he says. "Do you have any idea how dangerous the world is? Especially for someone with a raised profile as you will have. There is no way that you could ever safely navigate something like that. No. You must stay here."

"You said that I would be spearheading committees and—"

"Yes. In the palace. I have enemies, sparrow. You must be kept safe."

"You… You're talking about putting me in a cage."

"Yes. The cage will keep you safe. But look, look at these books. Look at this life. I can make you the most beautiful cage. You will not even see the bars."

I stare at him, and I know that he believes this is

true. I know that his arrogance makes it so that it seems impossible to him that I might not simply fall in line with what he wants. That I won't think this is the greatest idea devised by man or beast.

"All I will see is the bars, Lucian," I say.

He stares at me for a long moment, his expression turning to stone. "Then I will make them beautiful too."

And then he leaves me standing there, utterly bereft. All of my hope drained from me. I have to face the truth. I sold myself into marriage. And I have no control over anything.

I don't want to meet him for dinner. But the king has summoned me, and I'm told that I have no choice. I weigh my options. Because I know that I can refuse him. I can certainly stay in my room, force him to carry me down physically, or for him to get the guards to do so. I have more control than they want me to think. Because I can opt to be uncomfortable. I can opt to make it a war.

I decide not to, because I don't believe that it will help me. And as much as I would love to have a fight simply for the sake of it, I know there's no purpose to it.

I take a deep breath, and I begin to walk down the spiral staircase. Now I'm taking the stairs simply to prolong the amount of time it will take before I have to face him again.

When I walk in, he is sitting at the head of the table, looking thunderous. "You're late," he says.

"Yes, I am," I respond, and then take a seat two

chairs away from him, to be inflammatory, because I might not turn it into a war, but I may make it a small skirmish.

"I find you ungrateful," he says.

I am stunned into silence. All I can do is stare at him with my mouth dropped open. "You find…me… ungrateful?"

"Yes," he says. "You are entirely ungrateful. I had all those books sourced for you, and those shelves built in a mere few hours. You have any idea all the work that went into that?"

"You didn't do the work. Point me in the direction of the people on your staff who did it and I will send them a thank you."

"It was my idea," he says.

"It is also your idea to prevent me from doing the thing that I truly want to do with my life."

"It was your idea to submit yourself to this marriage," he says.

I can say nothing to that because he's correct, damn him.

"Would you like me to swap you out for your sister? Because there is still time. And if you think that I won't because of public perception, then I need you to stop and think about me. About all the things that I'm willing to let the public believe. Do you think that I care about my image?"

"I thought that this marriage was about improving your image."

"There's still time to commit a few acts of villainy before then, surely."

I don't know what to say to that. Because I don't want him to go and take my sister away from her happy life. Because I don't want…

I still don't want to trade places with her. And for some reason, the idea of leaving…

It makes me feel strange. Makes me feel like I would be leaving behind a project that I was in the middle of, and I really hate that thought, even if I don't understand why.

"Why do you care at all then?" I ask, my voice a near whisper.

I meet his gaze, those ice-blue eyes making me shiver. He makes me feel something I can't readily define and I don't know what to do with that at all. I want to run from him and draw closer at the same time.

"There is a time to move forward into the future," he says. "That time is now. Alabria needs more. Better. It can't happen as long as we're isolated."

"But you would keep me isolated."

"I would keep you safe."

"I don't want to be a prisoner."

"It isn't a prison."

"No. It's a cage. How is that different?"

"It is entirely different. Don't be disingenuous. If a bird flies free in the sky, it might be eaten by a hawk. But it can also be put into an aviary, and kept beautifully. Its life will be longer for its captivity. And it will be cared for."

"And will you clip its wings?"

"If the wings must be clipped in order to ensure its safety. Then yes."

"There is one problem, though. That means you think you know better than the bird. That you're smarter. Better. More powerful."

"If we're talking about you now, I don't believe that I'm smarter. But I do know more about this world that you find yourself in. I know more about the threats that exist out there."

"We aren't at war anymore," I say.

His face goes hard. "We do not need wars for death to find us." He says nothing for a long moment. "You know, I was tortured quite extensively when I was captured. And yes, it was a period of war. But I think you should know that there are people out there, regardless of their beliefs or what they attach themselves to, who simply enjoy inflicting pain. They attach their hatred to a cause, because then it makes them feel justified. But what they really enjoy is harming others. If one of those people were to get ahold of you, the things that they would do to you to get at me would be..." He touches the side of his face, and I can hear the gravity in his voice. "I hope that you never have any concept of what it feels like to experience your own skin melting. It is something you don't forget. Even thirty years later."

He speaks of it with such calm, matter-of-fact cool. Like he's talking about someone else. But I feel the impact of what he's saying like a gunshot.

I can't say anything, because what he's telling me is horrible. He would've been a boy thirty years ago. I knew that he hadn't been injured in a simple accident, and the scars are grotesque. But I didn't realize it was torture. I assumed it was some kind of explosion, battle injury. I didn't realize it was something so targeted. Something so…

"You are shocked. Because you think that I am the only thing in this country to be afraid of, but you are wrong. The press reports what the palace decided the world needed to know, and there were some things about me we've always decided were best…kept under wraps. That I was ever held captive was one of them."

"Why?" I ask, the word hushed.

"Who wants to know their leader is vulnerable?"

"So you let them think you're a monster?" I ask, and regret it. He looks at me with such ferocity I feel…

It isn't fear. My stomach is tight, my breathing shallow.

"It is true," he says. "We let it go a bit far. It is changing now." He gestures around the room. "I can keep you safe. But you have to let me."

"You want to keep me safe?"

"I have no desire to have to marry again. Two wives lost is one thing, three begins to look careless."

"It begins to look like murder is what it begins to look like," I say.

He laughs. "I didn't murder anyone. I know that severely impacts on my mystique. I won't tell you that I'm not a killer, because in the context of battle and self-defense, back in those days, I did what I had to do and more. But I have never harmed a woman."

I want to tell him that harm can be caused in more ways than just the physical. But I don't.

"I've survived this long, you should listen to me."

"I didn't know you until three days ago."

He inclines his head, a slight smile on his lips. And then we are interrupted again by dinner. I wish that I could hide my excitement for the food. But I can't.

"I do enjoy watching you eat," he says.

I wrinkle my nose when I look at him. "And why is that?"

"You take such obvious delight in it. It is exquisite. I told you, I wish to learn your favorites."

"I like this," I say, looking at the creamy pasta in front of me.

"And you enjoyed the cake."

"Yes," I say.

There is no point in being churlish about the food, because I do enjoy it, and I don't want him to serve me anything that I don't like. I have pride, but I also have to be somewhat realistic. And I don't want to be self-defeating.

"Tonight the cake is strawberry."

I do try to not look too pleased about that. Because there is a line between pleasure and humiliation. I don't wish to cross it.

But then, I never do. I try to keep my dreams manageable. Cerebral. Not emotional.

I'm pleased, though, by the mention of strawberry cake, and I try to hide my pleasure on principle.

He is looking at me in that way that he does. That way that makes me feel like my skin is covered with prickles. That way that makes me feel as if he can see straight inside of me.

I don't know how he's taken me from talking about my own captivity, trauma and war, to strawberry cake.

It's one of the ways in which I find him to be so dangerous, really. I can't anticipate him. My sister always accuses me of using my science brain when I'm being practical or analytical. I find that my science brain doesn't help me with Lucian. He doesn't behave in the way that I expect him to. He doesn't behave in quite the way I would expect anyone to.

He is frightening. But I don't get the sense that he's cruel. He's something. And he is certainly utterly implacable in the face of what I want. He doesn't mind looking me in the eye and telling me that he's putting me in a cage.

But I've been blunt with him from the very beginning. He, in return, is blunt with me. He claims, also, that he hasn't killed anyone. I do wonder why he's never denied it in the media. But then, he doesn't make announcements in the media. Apparently, he even suppresses the media.

Using my science brain, and maybe, also a little, my instincts, I decide that I'm going to be as direct with him as he is with me.

"I want my family to be present at our wedding party."

"Of course they will be. I will include your sister's fiancé, if you like."

"I would like," I say. "I would also like to be very clear that my family is going to be well compensated for all of this. That they'll always be taken care of."

"Obviously the family of the queen will not live in penury."

I scoff. "I wouldn't say that we do now. We are modest, but we do all right for ourselves."

"Silly little sparrow. You can't decide whether you want to have your pride or have a handout."

I'm offended by that as well. "I don't want a handout. But I had plans for my life." My voice catches. "I truly hoped that I was going to help benefit my family."

"And so you shall," he says.

"I think that we need more of the citizens of Alabria to come to this wedding. It cannot be something rarefied like you were planning on doing with Princess Emerald." I ignore the fact that maybe, maybe part of this is because I don't want the wedding to be exactly the same as the one he set into motion last year.

I don't know why it should matter to me. I don't need to be special to a maniacal dictator, after all. Except, I also know he isn't those things. But he is a puzzle that I can't quite work out.

"Make me your guest list, sparrow. I will give you whatever you wish."

"Except for my freedom."

He inclines his head. "Except for that, I regret."

The strawberry cake is served then, and I have to make a decision. Between my pride and my stomach. I choose my pride. I stand up from the table in front of the luscious pink piece of cake, and I look at him directly. "I'm going to bed. I find that I am extremely tired of the entire day."

And with that, I leave him. I half expect the dragon to follow me. But he doesn't.

There has been no blood spilled. It makes me wonder if this dragon even wants to be satiated at all.

Or if he is living for the game, for playing with his prey.

I, for certain, am his prey.

What the outcome of that will be, I don't know.

CHAPTER SIX

The Dragon

It never occurred to me that my little sparrow might be useful as a confessional. I have lived with my secrets, my thoughts, for so long. Yes, there are many in the palace who served under my parents who know pieces of truth about me, but no one knows me. When she asks me questions, I find that I want to answer them, however. When she pressed about my sins, I wanted to tell her that they were not quite as numerous as people have claimed.

But more than anything, I want to devour her.

More than anything, I must do something with the need that's building inside of me. More than I need this marriage, more than I need an heir. She is beautiful in ways I cannot fathom. Like the mysteries of the universe, a glorious, glimmering tangle in front of me. An entire galaxy of loveliness.

Soon she will be my wife. And I can have her in any way I like.

The only question is if I can wait that long.

Not even her defiance does anything to minimize my need for her. It only makes my hunger grow.

And I have never been one to ignore my appetite.

CHAPTER SEVEN

I HAVE NEVER liked parties. But here I am, dressed for one in which I am going to be the center, the focus. I put my hands on my stomach and look in the mirror. My hair is beautiful; my dress is the most glorious thing that I've ever seen.

Allison stands behind me and looks at me. "You are perfection."

I can't even dispute it. My hair is done in curls, with little golden butterflies clipped throughout, and the dress accentuates every asset I possess. All I can think of is the way that he looks at me. That icy gaze always watching. The tilt of his head. The sharp cut of his jaw, the ruined skin on his right, the perfection on his left.

What will he think of this?

I have never worried about such a thing. Whether or not a man found me beautiful. My stomach goes tight. I hate that I'm worrying about it now.

"Don't look so anxious," she says.

"I'm not used to things like this."

"No one is. It's a spectacle."

I can't argue with this. And I find myself somewhat mollified by the truth that everybody will be caught off guard by whatever it is that's happening. He's had one of these parties before, but not including the more common citizens of the country. And it didn't result in a wedding.

But ours will.

I'm not going to run away.

The certainty that I feel in that is frightening.

I have signed myself away. And I fully intend to follow through.

Whether or not I want to.

When I set my mind to something, I don't change it.

I gather up my courage, and look at myself one last time. "You are a miracle worker," I say to Allison. "I've never cared about my beauty because I didn't think it mattered. But…" I feel like I have to be honest, for the first time, even with myself. "My sister is much prettier than I am," I whispered. "It made it feel pointless to care overmuch about my looks."

"You are beautiful," Allison says. "Every woman is. And certainly is allowed to be vain."

I blink rapidly. I'm pleased that I've made this new friend, as alien as the entire situation is.

"Thank you."

Though, as I walk from my chambers to the ballroom, I can't help but wonder how I'll fare when compared to my sister. She'll be there tonight. It doesn't take a team of people to make her look stunning.

And I feel awful, because Eve and I have never been in competition with each other. We have always gotten along very well, we've wanted different things and that has served us well.

But she was once intended to marry Lucian. Now I am. So I can't help but feel as if I will be put in direct comparison to her.

In some traditions Lilith is the first wife of Adam. Eve is ultimately his chosen bride.

What if he sees her and changes his mind? What if he sees what everyone does? That she's the real beauty.

If she were to see Lucian…

If she saw what I did.

And if she wanted him? Why would that matter to you?

I think of the entire room filled with science books, my beautiful, well-designed cage. Why do I suddenly feel reluctant to leave it? And him?

Suddenly, I am being swarmed by staff members. All fussing over me as they lead me toward the ballroom. "You will be announced," his chief aide says to me. "And you will be on your own."

I imagine all of those people looking at me and I freeze. The very idea fills me with dread.

But then suddenly, the double doors to the ballroom are opening, and I am being ushered in. And there I am, at the top of the stairs, hundreds of faces turned toward me.

I can find my center. I should look for my mother. My sister.

But my eyes find him. He is looking at me. Those ice-blue eyes are filled with intensity. His jaw is clenched, and so are his hands, held at his sides in fists.

I can't take my eyes off of him. I don't know if he makes me feel grounded or more terrified. I don't know if I want him to keep looking at me or if I want him to turn away.

I take a deep, gasping breath. Dimly I'm aware that my name has been spoken. The people are clapping. I hate this. I feel dizzy. I was never made to be in front of people. I've never wanted to be. And then, he's ascending the stairs, coming toward me. That wasn't part of what we discussed. It wasn't part of what they told me. I was supposed to walk down to him. But he's coming to me. He extends his hand, and I take it.

I'm ashamed of the feeling that washes through me. Intense. Earth-shattering.

This isn't scientific. It's visceral. I was so convinced I'd survive here by using my wits, and that I'd figure him out. Instead I've managed to make myself into a puzzle.

He holds my hand in his and begins to lead me down the steps, into the ballroom. I find that I want to lean against him. To hide against the vast, muscled wall of his chest, let him wrap his arms around me and keep me shielded.

My jailer. My protector. I've never felt the two things quite so strongly. People are still clapping, and they're looking at me like they're pleased with me. But I still can't find my center. I feel out of body. And it is the feeling of his strong, calloused hands around mine that brings me back to the moment.

In the middle of that crowded room, we stop, he takes my other hand and looks at me. I'm lost. Held captive in this arcing current between us. Lucian.

And then suddenly I feel hands on my shoulder, and

I release my hold on him in turn. My sister is there, gripping me, looking at me excitedly. “Oh, Lilith,” she says. “You look extraordinary.”

I look back at Lucian, who is gazing at my sister as if she is a creature from another planet.

“This is Eve,” I say. “Eve,” I say and direct my sister toward him, “this is Lucian.”

“Goodness,” she says, looking all the way up at him, and I fight the urge to step in front of him. I don’t know why. Whether I want to protect him from the reaction that my sister might have to his scars, or whether I just don’t want her all that close to him.

“He’s the king,” I remind her.

I look at Lucian, who seems amused. He finds it so funny when people are scared of him. But I’m not entirely sure that Eve is scared of him so much as in awe. His presence is magnetic; that can’t be denied.

Soon, my mother joins us. “Your Highness,” she says, barely able to look up at him. “It is such an honor to meet you. And such an honor that you have chosen my…my daughter to marry.”

Lucian chuckles. “Yes,” he says, drawing his arm around my waist and bringing me in close to him. “I have chosen her.” He touches my face, wrapping a curl around his finger, and I shiver.

I’m not sure if he’s making a mockery of the situation. Of how he *had* chosen Eve, and then I stepped in, or if he is trying to reinforce the fact that I’m with him now. I hate that it makes me feel insecure. But it makes me feel less. I have always felt so firmly rooted in my world. The things that I’m good at. I’ve never felt like I had to compete with Eve. I don't like the feeling now. I wonder if everybody in attendance is looking at us and thinking how I suffer in comparison to her. Because yes, as I feared, she is glorious. Her red hair is riotous and lovely, her voluptuous figure showed off to perfection by the green dress she's wearing. She is so like Princess Emerald.

The other woman that he intended to marry.

His obvious and actual type.

I've seen pictures of his late wives. All of them were beautiful. Perfection. Much more like Eve than like me. Birds of paradise when compared to a small sparrow.

I blink, and try to hold back tears of indignation and insecurity. And rage. It is no small amount rage that I am being forced to care about this thing that I've spent my entire life not caring about at all.

And that it's happening to me in such a public space. On a stage.

"Where's Marcus?" I ask.

"He's somewhere," Eve says, giggling. "But I wanted to talk to my sister anyway. What a lovely party this is." I look around the room, at the fairy-tale nature of it. The twisted golden branches adorning everything. Fairy lights all around. There is something romantic about it. There is something strangely *romantic* about Lucian. I've never been romantic. He bought me all those books. He's trying to share his fiction with me.

I'm lost in that thought for a moment, before I snap myself back to the moment on a deep breath. "Yes," I agree. "It's beautiful."

Lucian is waylaid by dignitaries, and I find myself

being dragged around the room by Eve, who seems to have made friends with half of the attendees. She sparkles, and everyone around her shimmers in response.

Over the next two hours I meet more people than I think I've ever met in my life.

"You would've been good at this," I say softly when Eve and I are alone for a moment.

"Oh, but what a beast he is," she says. "I mean… he's quite gorgeous."

Something possessive rises up inside of me. "He's not a beast," I say. "And I don't think he ever killed anyone."

"You don't?" Eve asks.

I watch her to see if that makes her…regret her choice. If she'll regret choosing Marcus over the king. She doesn't seem to, at all.

"Lilith, is he good to you?"

"He's…" I try to find the words for Lucian. I barely know him, and yet…he has told me so much about himself. I've shared with him. He built me the bookshelves. He wants to know my favorite food. He's obsessed with me eating, with pleasing me in certain fashions.

I'm in a situation I chose, even though the circumstances were narrow, and I felt a little like a lab rat in a maze. Like I had options, but they were dead ends. Or ends that resulted with one of the other rats being unhappy, anyway.

"He's good to me," I say. "I think… I think he might even be kind in his way."

Eve's eyes are shining. "Do you like him?"

"I…" I have no idea how to answer the question. I

find him infuriating. He is bound and determined to own me. To prevent me from realizing my dreams. He is also the most compelling, magnetic man that I have ever known. But there's nothing easy about him. Nothing half so pastoral as simple *liking.*

"Have you slept with him?"

Eve is extremely keen on the question, and I feel heat wash through my body.

"*No,*" I say.

Eve makes a comedically dramatic expression. "That is a pity. Because he looks like he's good for *that.*"

I have so many questions, since this is the prevailing opinion of the two women I've talked to who have actual sexual experience when it comes to Lucian.

I know that when I look at him, it makes me feel hot. I know that his touch sets off a chain reaction inside me I can't control.

But I don't know *why.*

I need one of these women with sexual experience to give me some actual details.

After that, I am passed around the room, introduced to more people than I can count. And Lucian is across the room from me, but I can't seem to get to him. To cross this wave of people. Then, I lose track of my sister, even, and I'm just left out there to drown in the social ocean. I swallow hard, and slip back to the edge of the room. The crowd of people folds in, and for a moment, nobody's looking at me.

Nothing has prepared me for this.

None of the skills that I've cultivated.

I take my opportunity, and sneak out. There's a door

to the garden, and I melt away, invisible. That's something that I'm good at. The studious one. The bookish one. I'm good at not being seen.

Except, in all this gold, with the butterflies in my hair, I am much more conspicuous than I've ever been.

Belonging to Lucian, I'm much more conspicuous than I have ever been.

I swallow hard, walking away from the palace. I don't even know where I'm going. The evening is warm, and my hair is heavy on the back of my neck. The breeze smells of gardenia, jasmine and other glorious flowers. I can't see, but I know they're there. The moon is full, the sky scattered full of stars. I close my eyes and allow the warm breeze to filter across my skin. I allow myself a moment of tranquility.

A moment to remember who I am.

Except, even that moment doesn't really help. Because less than a week ago, I was university-bound, and I had never experienced feelings even half as conflicting as the ones I felt tonight. A strange kind of possessiveness for a man who's holding me captive. Jealousy. The feeling of being the center of attention. All of these things are as far removed from the me that I know as any stranger could be.

There is a hedge maze, and I dip inside, wandering through the twists and turns before I find a stone bench. I sit down, and put my hand on my chest. Feel my heart beating.

I know who I am.

I tell myself that. And still, I can seem to find a way to ground myself.

"Sparrow."

I hear his voice, and everything in my body responds to it. Responds to him. As though I'm relieved to see my captor, as though I wish to be back in my cage. I am momentarily immobilized by how much I despise that. By how much I despise myself, but then he comes around the corner, and I see something genuinely like fear on his face. The moonlight illuminates his blond hair, his eyes so pale they're almost white.

"What are you doing out here?"

"I just needed a break."

"I thought you ran away. Or perhaps worse, had harmed yourself."

He's expressed worry about that twice, and I can't help but wonder why. I already know he's nothing like any of the rumors suggest. He's interesting. He has the soul of a poet, and the body of a warrior. He has the ruthlessness of a warrior too, but people can contain multitudes.

He cares about my happiness—unless what I want makes him unhappy. He definitely cares about his own more.

He's a mystery.

"I'm not going to hurt myself," I say.

"I didn't know," he says. He moves close to me, and he drops down to his knees in front of me. He's close, and as glorious as the garden smells, he's better. My heart is thundering so hard it's the loudest sound for me right now. My mouth is dry; my body is on high alert. And my science brain is nowhere to be found.

He reaches up and touches my face, his thumb tracing the outline of my lower lip. "Do not run from me," he says, his voice rough. "I thought you ran away."

I shake my head. "I gave you my word, Lucian. I'm not a liar."

He breathes out, a sigh that almost sounds like relief. "Yes. That is true." Then he shifts his hold on me, his hand going to cup my cheek, the hold possessive, firm. My heart is beating hard still, but this isn't fear. It's different. My chest aches, the sensation more of a throb right at the center of my breastbone. And then, more disturbing, I feel an answering throb at the center of my thighs. I can't help but think about what my sister said. That he looks like he would be good at sex. I've never given that a thought. Certainly Eve knows what sort of man might be good at it.

I wouldn't. I would have nothing to compare it to, and very few fantasies to even call up and try to apply his image to. And yet I'm not so foolish that I don't understand what's happening to my body. His closeness is…is making me want him.

Want.

What a strange thought. Me wanting this man. This man who is holding me captive. This man who seemed *scared* at the idea that I might've run from him.

He releases his hold on me, and turns his attention to my ankle. He wraps his large hand around it, lifts it up and rests my foot against his chest.

"What?"

I can't conjure a thought or get out a sentence, because he begins to push my dress up my legs, revealing my bare skin to the night air. He adjusts my leg, puts it up on his shoulder and begins to draw closer as he pushes my dress up higher. My eyes go wide, and he inserts himself between my thighs, pressing my other leg out far, my dress now up all the way, so that he's staring at the golden underwear that I put on before the dress. The underwear is very pretty, but I've never had anyone look at me like this, and I feel nothing but embarrassment. I'm a liar.

I don't *only* feel embarrassment. He looks up at me, his gaze hungry, and I'm sure he sees hunger mirrored in mine. But also wonder, confusion. Fear. I don't want him to stop, though. I want him to keep going. I want him to show me.

I want him to solve this puzzle for me.

Then he puts his hand on my bare thigh, drawing his fingertip to the sensitive skin at the crease, pushing beneath the fabric of my panties.

My breath catches as he grazes my most intimate flesh. He growls, a sound of satisfaction rumbling in his chest. He's never kissed me. Right as I think that, he leans in and kisses my inner thigh. The sensation is like a shock wave through my body.

"Let me show you why you should stay with me," he says, kissing his way up toward that golden triangle between my legs, ripping the fabric to the side, and closing his mouth over my flesh. He takes no quarter, and I can't believe the intimacy that he's claiming. His tongue slides through my folds, moves ruthlessly over the sensitive bundle of nerves there. And I can't help but react.

My hips fly up off the bench, and he wraps his free

arm around me, drawing me tighter against his mouth as he continues to lick me. Until he's devouring me like the dragon that I feared him to be. The pleasure is otherworldly. Like nothing I've even imagined. I thought that because I knew how to bring myself to the peak that I understood something about sexual pleasure. But I don't. Because in that situation I was always in control of it. How fast, how intense. I have no control here. It's all him. His wicked lips, his tongue. I hear the sounds of pleasure that he's making, pleasure that's coming from tasting me. There.

I have no choice but to surrender. I'm lost. Lost to reality. Lost to the earth itself. I might as well be among the stars.

I hear the sound of my panties tearing, pulled entirely free of my body. Then with both hands, he grips my rear and holds me against his mouth as he consumes me. He shifts, putting his hand between my legs, using it in conjunction with his tongue before he pushes two fingers deep inside of me, the pain and pleasure mixing, along with the unfamiliar sensation of deep penetration, sending me right over the edge.

My internal muscles squeeze tight around his fingers as I cry out with pleasure. With abandon. Without care that someone might hear. I find a hand over my mouth then as I continue to ride the wave. He pulls me from the bench, onto his lap, holds me against him, keeps his hand firmly pressed on my mouth as the aftershocks continue on through my body.

"Don't announce it, sparrow," he whispers against my head.

"I didn't mean to," I whisper.

"Are you a virgin, sweet sparrow?"

My throat tightens, and I find myself fighting tears. "Virginity isn't even a real thing," I say. "The idea that a man's member has the power to change a woman is incredibly regressive."

"It's not so simple," he whispers against my hair. "It is not about a man having the power to change a woman. What I want to know is if you've ever been this close to anyone else. If you've ever felt pleasure like that. If anyone has ever touched you there, tasted you there."

"Why?" I ask. I feel small, and I feel like weeping.

"The fact that you won't tell me gives me all the information I need."

We're silent for a long moment. Then he stands, and deposits me firmly on the ground. "Come. Let us return to the party. People will be wondering where we are."

"I can't… I can't see anyone… They'll know."

He bends down and picks something up off the grass. I realize it's my underwear. He puts them in his pocket, his eyes never leaving mine, and I know a terrible lashing of shame. I didn't resist him at all. Not even for a moment. I didn't try to pull away. I didn't try to do anything but receive pleasure from him.

I just didn't think this was who I was. I didn't think I was subject to these same needs and desires as my mom, as my sister. I love them both but they've thrown themselves into love affairs at the expense of themselves. They've let men determine how happy they'll be and I think it's because of the power sex has to cloud your mind.

I just didn't think I was like that.

I thought I was a scientist, not a sensualist.

Nonfiction, not fiction.

Not a romantic.

And yet now I feel like I've been lit on fire with the possibility of this. Of him.

I feel like I want to know things I didn't before. I feel like he's changed me, and that feels shameful.

Yet, I can't stop it.

"I don't care if everyone knows," he says.

"Why not?"

"You're going to be my wife. Better that I desire you, isn't that correct?"

I want to ask him questions about that. If he really wants me or if I was convenient. If he was simply manipulating me with pleasure because it was a convenient thing for him to do. I think he knows that I'm a virgin. It would be so easy for him to find the information out empirically.

I've never been on a date. Never even been close.

He could have easily found that out if he'd asked the right people. Therefore, he must have known how easy it would be to completely blindside me with desire like that.

But he is leading me back into the ballroom, so I can ask him that. I can say any of the things that I want to say. Tomorrow, I'm marrying this man. And I've just been given a taste of what need feels like with him.

My own lack of control terrifies me. More than he

ever has. The one thing that surprises me above all else is that I'm no longer most afraid of Lucian.

I'm afraid of myself.

CHAPTER EIGHT

It's the day of the wedding, and I didn't sleep well. After the ball, Lucian disappeared. It was like nothing ever happened between us out in the garden. He didn't pursue anything else; he didn't ask me any more questions. I went back to my room, and I went to sleep. I kept waking up, expecting for him to be there in the corner. But he wasn't.

And then, worst of all, when I finally did go to sleep I kept waking up aching and sweating, thinking about the way that he took my body and made it his.

I don't even have time to think about it; I don't have time to worry about it. Because then early in the morning I'm dragged out of bed by Allison and her team, and I am wrapped in the beautiful, custom-made wedding gown that has been worked on morning and night for me.

The satin is heavy, glimmering, a glorious candlelight color that flatters me in a way that nothing else has. Even I have to admit that I'm a beautiful bride, but I wonder how much of that has to do with the way that I feel in my body today. It's like I feel more in touch with myself than I ever have. Like I'm aware of every part of myself. Every dip and hollow and curve. And why each one exists.

I'm furious with myself. Because as I told him last night, the idea that the touch of a man turns a woman from an innocent into anything else fills me with rage. Yet I also feel as if I learned something about myself last night.

If I had been asked my feelings on being…on having… If I'd had to give a dissertation on my feelings regarding oral sex I would have said that it seemed vaguely distasteful to me. He made it seem perfectly reasonable. More than that, it was one of the more incredible sights I've seen, that large, powerful man kneeling between my legs tasting me like I was the dessert.

But the result is that I feel like a stranger in my own body, and even my thoughts feel like they belong to a stranger, because the Lilith that I was a week ago would never have thought such a thing. And certainly wouldn't have been thinking about when he might do it again.

Particularly not ahead of such a life-changing event. How could an orgasm rewire my brain like this? I should be thinking about the wedding. About the fact that I was officially committing myself to this, and to him, not about the way it felt to have his hands on my bare skin, for his tongue to explore my body in such an intimate way.

I gasp, and look away from the mirror. "I'm ready," I say.

The trouble is, it's not time for the wedding to start

yet. I find myself alone in a small room waiting. Waiting and waiting. I crack open the door and look out, and for the first time I realize there are guards there. He's afraid that I'm going to run away. Still. He doesn't trust me. Apparently, my word wasn't enough for him, and I find that excessively outrageous given the fact that he had his mouth between my legs.

"Are you making sure I don't run away?" I ask the guards.

"And that no one comes to rescue you," the guard returns, and I wonder if he used the word *rescue* by accident. It seems that *kidnapped* or *stolen* would be more appropriate, unless he fears the king as well, and thinks that I might need a rescue.

It's amazing to me that I no longer think that.

Finally, it's time for the wedding to start, and I am ushered from the tiny room and to the doors of the sanctuary. I walk down the aisle by myself. There is no one to give me away. But my mother and sister and her fiancé are sitting in the front row, looking happy and proud. I avoid looking at Lucian. I avoid it until the very last moment. And then, when I can do it no longer, he takes my hand and our eyes collide.

"Sparrow," he whispers.

I can't say anything. My throat is too tight. And as the priest presides over the wedding ceremony, Lucian continues to watch not only me but the audience. The priest. Everyone. I know that his last bride was carried away, and he seems like he's anticipating it happening again.

I swallow hard, and I don't take my eyes off of his. I

make my vows with an unwavering voice, and I'm not sure where that comes from. I'm not sure how I manage it. And then, the priest says that it's time for us to kiss. We've never done that.

He has touched my face, he has licked me between my legs, but he's never kissed my mouth.

And then, he leans in, and captures my lips. I am overcome. His mouth is a conqueror. Claiming me, my body, my mind. He thrusts his tongue deep into my mouth, and I capitulate to him, allowing him entry. He wraps his arms around me, drawing me up against his large body, and I cling to him.

Lucian.

His lips are a revelation. Kissing him is an entirely new experience. I don't know how many more new experiences I can possibly take, and yet I know there are more before me. I've married him. Kissing him should not be the biggest aspect of the moment. Yet I find that it is. His hold on me is hard, uncompromising, and I don't want to resist it. I want him to cling to me forever.

I want to cling to him.

But then, it's over, and I find myself searching the audience for my sister, my mother. But I'm dizzy. He takes my hand and leads me down the aisle, his steps firm and decisive. And we are walking toward the tower.

"Lucian," I whisper. "Isn't there a reception?"

"We had that last night. That's what the wedding party was."

"It…it was?"

"I find myself impatient to spend time with my new bride."

My heart moves up to my throat. "Oh?"

"Yes. There will be a party for everyone in attendance, but as I have managed to keep my bride this time… We will be consummating as quickly as possible."

I gasp, and he doesn't stop.

Even now, he doesn't take the elevator. Even now, he takes me up the stairs, turning and turning, climbing ever upward, my heart in my throat, and my entire body giddy with adrenaline. I don't know why, but I make a small game of guessing which room he'll take me to. Mine or his. It's better than guessing what's going to happen. Better than obsessing about what's to come.

It's midmorning. Not long ago I was put into this dress. I didn't expect the wedding night to happen in the middle of the day. I thought there would be a whole wedding party, a whole prelude.

The prelude, I suppose, has been this entire week. What happened last night in the garden was foreplay.

It'll be a relief, to have it over with. To know what it's like. To see him naked. To know what it is to have a man…

I take a sharp breath and then I find myself at the threshold of his room. I've never been there before. It makes sense, of course, that he would choose to do it here. Not in the space that I've grown so accustomed to, but in his domain.

He looks at me, just there in front of the door,

reaches out and takes hold of my chin with his thumb and forefinger. "Are you ready for me?"

I'm not sure what to make of the question. I was expecting a claiming. And I certainly wasn't expecting him to look at me with…tenderness. Yes. That's the expression on his face. I don't know what to say. I don't know how to speak. It's like I can't access my brain at all now. It's like nothing I've ever experienced before.

"Sweet girl," he murmurs.

I feel very strongly that I should not react to that. That his words shouldn't send a shock of pleasure through me. But they do. Then he opens the door to his room and leads me inside slowly.

"Get on the bed," he says. My world narrows, and I can't take in the entire scope of his room. So I obey him. I walk to the bed and I sit at the foot of it, my eyes trained on him. "Very good," he says.

He begins to take his clothes off. The black tie he's wearing, the white shirt. He sheds it along with his coat, and reveals his heavily muscled body. There are scars all over his torso. Burns, terrible like the ones on his face, cuts, twisting through his well-defined muscles. But he's incredibly beautiful. Mesmerizing. I know that every mark on his flesh tells the story, and I find myself hungry then to hear it.

Even though I know it speaks of pain. I want to know his pain.

He's my husband.

My husband. The word echoes within me.

He moved his hands to his belt, and undoes it slowly. He sheds the rest of his clothes with ease. There is no hesitation. No discomfort. He isn't embarrassed, and he has nothing to be embarrassed of. His body is a study in masculine perfection. I may have nothing to compare it to, but I am aware that I'm in the presence of a magnificent specimen.

It's like years' worth of desire has flooded me. Like all the things that I've repressed all this time, kept myself from thinking of because I've been so laser focused on the future that I can no longer have, crash in.

I can't have university. I won't get my degree. I won't do medical research.

But I will be the Queen of Alabria. I will be King Lucian's wife. And now he's going to claim me. He's going to show me what sex is like. He's going to give me more pleasure, I'm certain, judging by the look on his face. But he's also going to…

He is a very large man. Everywhere. I think back to what Allison said to me that first day we met. About how he's certainly proportional.

She wasn't wrong.

He's also extremely aroused. From looking at me.

From anticipating touching me.

I don't think I've ever felt half so powerful in my life as I do right then. Which is so strange, because I'm at a disadvantage. He has taken me upstairs, closed me in his room. He's the one with knowledge and experience that far outstrip mine. He's older than me. He's lived many lifetimes, been married before.

Twice before.

I'm the one who until last night had never been touched intimately by another person.

But he wants me.

Even if it's only the biological reaction a male has to seeing a female, I am powerful as a woman, even if I am not singular.

Even if it's only because of my gender.

That is power, real all the same.

I shift, not quite sure what to do, moving as if maybe I should take my dress off. He shakes his head. "I will remove your clothes. You will not do anything, do you understand me? My sweet, virgin sparrow, this is about you. I'm going to teach you. Everything you need to know about pleasure. Everything you need to know to want to stay with me."

I nod, my heart pounding hard, my ears buzzing. He moves toward me, his gaze intent on mine, and then he grips my waist, turning me sharply on the bed so that my back is to him. He leans in and kisses my shoulder, and I shiver. He unzips the back of my dress and lets it fall away. He strips it away from me as if it weighs nothing, as if it isn't a massive, complicated ball gown. And I feel a hollow ache at the center of my chest.

I'm the third bride that he's undressed.

For some reason, that makes me feel sad. For some reason, it steals some of my life. Some of my power.

"What is it?" His lips are close to my ear. He isn't even looking at my face. I don't know how he knows that I've upset myself.

"Nothing," I whisper, anticipation and fear warring with my emotions. Part of me just wants to get this over with. So that it isn't something I don't know anymore. So that it isn't something I have to fear.

"Don't lie to me. It's very important that we have trust. I'm naked, sparrow. You are about to be. If I ask you something I need to know that you're telling me the truth. I need to know I can trust you to tell me if something doesn't feel good for you. If you don't want something. I'm a man," he says, letting his knuckles drift down my bare back, the sensation pleasurable. "And I want you. Viciously. I need to know that it's safe for me to give in to that desire. I have to be able to trust you to be honest."

"You've done this before," I say. I don't bother to clarify that I mean the wedding and not sex.

"Yes," he says. His voice softens. "Does that bother you?"

"I was just thinking of all the other wedding dresses you've removed."

He nods. I can feel it. "The first one was twenty years ago."

"Yes. I know."

"I have lived more life than you. That means I have a past. But you will be my future."

We don't talk about the second wife. We don't talk about the third one he tried to have. He might not have had a third wife, but he had a third whole wedding.

His words, though, do something to soothe the ache inside of me. I am surprised by the revelations of the past two days. I want to feel special more than I realized. I blink back tears, and he kisses my neck. The feel of him touching me helps banish my sadness. And then, I find myself getting lost. His mouth moves over my tender skin. His hands begin to skim over my curves, going to cup my breasts. He pulls my bra down, exposing my breasts, those rough hands now against my skin. Then he lifts his hand and turns my face, capturing my mouth again. This kiss is slow, unhurried but no less deep than the one that we shared during the ceremony. He makes quick work of stripping the rest of my garments away, leaving me naked on the bed. He moves away from me, and I find that without him touching me I begin to feel panicked again. But he is in no hurry. He looks at me, taking almost methodical stock of my body.

He makes a low, growling sound, wrapping his hand around his arousal and pumping himself twice, my throat drying at the sight. "You should give thanks for my experience," he says. "Because I know you need me to be slow. And I have the patience. A boy in his twenties would have claimed you by now, and spent his seed. He would've given you no pleasure, and a lot of pain. I promise I won't."

Then he joins me on the bed, cupping my face and kissing me again. Kissing me and kissing me, his tongue sliding against mine. He moves his hand between my legs, and begins to stroke me. Pleasure building low in my stomach. He pushes a finger inside of me, and begins to stroke me there. Adding a second finger as I grow wetter and wetter.

The pleasure within me is now bigger than my discomfort. His body is large and hot, and I have that strong desire to melt into him again, even as his fingers sink inside me, over and over. Building need within me that matches and even exceeds what I felt last night in the garden. And then, I reach my peak, shaking and trembling, while he looks into my eyes, while he seems to stare into my soul. He kisses my mouth again, then down my neck, his lips skimming over my nipple as he kisses down my body and finds my center again just like he did last night. And he devours me. I think that I cried his name out. Or maybe it's only an inarticulate noise. I grab his shoulders, trying to hang onto him. I'm dimly aware that I'm digging my nails into him.

That I've scratched him. While he licks into me like I'm an ice cream. I'm already raw, sensitive from my recent climax, and he's pushing me toward the edge again. He isn't asking me to climax again. He's demanding it. His tongue is merciless, and I hold onto him so hard I'm quite certain that I've drawn blood as I cried out his name.

I look at his skin, his shoulders. Drops of red. I'm the one that's drawn blood. Before the dragon had a chance.

Perhaps it's his blood that speaks to the satisfaction of the maiden. Though then I looked down at the most masculine part of him, and I'm reminded that I have yet to bleed.

If this were medieval times, he would be hanging the sheet out the window of the turret, announcing his conquest of my virginity.

And I'm sure there will be ample evidence of it.

He keeps his eyes on me, and pushes his fingers into his own mouth, licking them clean as he watches for my reaction.

I shiver, and he holds me against him. Kissing me

slowly and softly. And he lays me down on the bed, positioning his body just so, the head of his arousal against the entrance to my body. "This will hurt," he says roughly. "But I promise you, I will make it worth it all the nights after."

He presses into me, slowly, stretching me. I find my body giving to accommodate him. But as he goes deeper and deeper, his length stretching me, I find myself whimpering. He kisses me, swallows my cry of pain as he thrusts deep. And then he just holds me, like that. Buried deep within me. This man who was a stranger a week ago. I'm bewildered by the thought. Overcome by it. Because how can that be? How is it that I didn't know Lucian even seven days ago? And now he's inside of me. Blood that I've drawn on his shoulders, the flavor of my pleasure on his tongue. There is something so deeply uncivilized about this. And I've surrendered to it. More than that, I participated in it.

Then he kisses me, and all of my thoughts vanish. He begins to move inside of me and the discomfort begins to fade, transforming into something beautiful. I can feel each stroke, every inch, and it's glorious. More than that, there is a deep, possessive certainty within me. I might be his. But he's mine. And perhaps that's the real change. Not so much that he's taken my virginity, but that he's given me this understanding.

That it isn't simply my body that belongs to him. His belongs to me. Yes, he's taken other women out of their wedding dresses. He's probably deflowered other virgins. Part of his lore is how he's rough and brilliant in bed—a monster, true, but a sensual talent.

I don't care now, though. Because there is no room for any of that in this moment.

We are as close as two people can be.

How extraordinary, yet again, that this enigma of a man now knows me in ways no one else ever has.

And I know him.

I watch his face as his movements begin to pick up pace, as those measured thrusts become fractured. As the control leaves him. He's mine. My captive in that moment. Everything that I felt when he kissed me, touched me, licked me, he feels now. I try to hang onto my control. I try not to give in to the rising tide of pleasure within me. Because I want him to be undone when I am in control. I want to feel the same satisfaction he must've felt. But I can't fight the desire he's creating inside of me. That sweet friction deep within me.

"Please," he grits out. "Come for me, beautiful girl."

And I do. Because he asked. Because he said please. And I am undone by such an arrogant man begging.

I arch my back against his and cry out, and his own roar follows mine, as he spills himself deep inside of me.

I've given my freedom away. It wasn't the vows that did it. It was this.

I let him come inside of me.

I've surrendered my freedom for a taste of pleasure. I didn't worry about protection at all, and I could get pregnant. But it wasn't a concern, not when I was so desperate for me. And as he lingers over me, looking at me, I want to regret it. But I can't. I have always felt like maybe I was smarter than other people, and it was my compensation for the poverty I was born into. I have a brain that can think me out of so many situations. One that was going to take me straight to university, out of this country. But in this, I am just like everyone else. I've given everything away for a taste of sexual desire.

I am no better than anyone.

I thought I was more sensible than my sister because I'm not a romantic, but isn't it worse to have surrendered to need without even a promise of romance?

But then he wraps me in his arms, and I feel something like romance. My heart begins to expand inside of my chest, and I want to believe that this expression of tenderness is care, and not just manipulation.

But then, I find myself getting so sleepy. And I don't want to think anymore. Thinking isn't a comfort. I just want sleep. And for Lucian to hold me.

I surrender to my feelings. And I let my thoughts drift away.

CHAPTER NINE

I WAKE UP on a gasp, sitting and clutching the bedclothes to my chest. My naked chest. I'm in Lucian's room, in the center of his gigantic bed. It's dark outside, and I'm alone.

A sob rises up in my throat, and I lie down, trying to get ahold of myself. There's no reason to be hysterical.

There is certainly no reason to cry. I chose everything that happened today.

Tears gather in my eyes and I close them. My stomach growls, and I feel so alone. I'm not sure if I'm grateful that he's left me or…

The door opens. I stay lying like that, not giving any indication that I'm awake.

"Sparrow?"

I stir just slightly.

"I have something for you."

I open my eyes.

"Are you hungry?"

"Yes," I say softly.

"I have something for you to dress in, darling."

Darling. I hold that close, turn it over, try to examine it. Is it sweet and lovely because it's not that strange nickname he calls me? Is it personal or is it something he has called every other woman he's married?

He moves to the bed, wrapping me in the softest robe I've ever felt against my skin, and touches my cheek. "You were lovely tonight."

The simple compliment takes me aback. I blink, trying to catch my breath.

Then I find myself being lifted from the bed. "You don't have to carry me," I say.

"I want to," he says.

He carries me out of the bedroom, and to the elevator. "Oh, come on now. When I'm not walking you don't take the stairs?"

"I will not gamble with your safety," he growls, closing the elevator door, still holding me while it descends. I loop my arms around his neck, hold onto him until it reaches its destination. The doors open, and he sweeps me out, down the hall into the dining room. My jaw drops. He sets me gently down, and I move deeper into the room. The lights are off, but the table is covered in candles. Held high in golden candelabras, and there is a feast laid out before me. Dishes that I don't have names for. Things that look exotic and familiar. Gourmet foods, and comfort foods. And besides that, behind the banquet table, an entire spread of dessert.

"This is… Are we expecting an army?"

"Only you and I," he says.

"Then why…why all this?"

"Because you deserve it," he says. "And I wanted to give it to you."

I walk down the length of the table, looking at all of

the bounty. And I sit down, unsure of where to start. He picks up a large plate. "What can I serve for you?"

"I don't know," I say.

And he begins to pile the plate high. With a bit of everything. He sets it before me, and moves to sit next to me. He tucks my hair behind my ear, and kisses my neck. I don't know what to do with this. With this side of him. This sweetness and care. Except, something inside of me cautions me. Lucian does not have a reputation for being kind. Not in any capacity. Whatever this is, it's more of the same. More of him trying to convince me that I am happy in my cage.

I can't afford to forget that. But I take my first bite of the meal, and it's so glorious that I do let myself set my worries aside for the moment.

Because they won't change anything.

I eat ham and mashed potatoes. Pastas with sauces that I can't identify. Orzo dishes, feta and olives. Roast chicken, steak and the nicest vegetables I've ever seen. And then it's time for desserts.

"Strawberry," he says. "I owe you a piece of strawberry cake. When you are not mad at me."

I'm not mad at him now; that is true. Though I do feel lightheaded, and on guard. I'm trying not to feel too satisfied. Or too happy.

Because part of me feels like I have to resist this. Even though I've made the choice. Part of me feels like it's a betrayal of the dreams that I used to have, to allow myself to be happy with him when he's laid down an edict that I don't like or accept.

But then, if I'm not a romantic, surely I should be

able to separate my feelings from my thoughts. The feelings in my body from emotional feelings. Surely.

Except, he is waging a war, not just on my body, but everything. Because this is nothing if not psychological warfare.

But I eat the strawberry cake anyway, and it's wonderful.

And then when he leans in close and asks me, "What is your favorite?"

He steals my breath with his beauty. And I let him kiss me, rather than even trying to answer the question. He strokes my face, my hair, kisses my lips, down my neck. Then he parts my robe, cupping my breast, right there in the dining room, like we're in a locked room, like we don't have the chance of being interrupted at any moment.

He growls, undoing the belt on my robe and opening it entirely, his chair facing mine, as he looks at me, his eyes feral as he takes in the sight of my naked body. I do have power.

That is the truth.

It wasn't something that I hallucinated up there in our room.

His desire for me is pushing him; it's making him act like this.

The one thing I don't know is if he's always like this. I need to see a crack in his armor. I need to know.

He overwhelmed me upstairs, his lips, his hands making me forget all of my questions. But I have the advantage of having had three orgasms only recently, and as much as I want him again, I am sustained by the recency of my pleasure.

"I need to know," I say. "Is this your wedding night routine? Have you brought all of your virgin brides to three sobbing climaxes before bringing them to a feast?"

"No," he says.

"Did you want them all like you want me?"

"Never," he says. "I have wanted no woman the way that I want you."

That doesn't feel true. It doesn't feel like it can be. But if he feels that way now, that I'm willing to suspend my disbelief. Because if that's what he thinks, then what does the truth matter? If he doesn't remember how strongly he wanted the other women, then that's just as good, isn't it? At least, that's what I want to believe. Even while I'm frustrated with myself that I need it.

But the truth is, the need he creates in me has overtaken me to such a degree, has turned me into such a stranger to my own self, that I need to know he's suffering from it too. I need to know that I'm not alone.

The light in his eyes, like a fire, tells me that I'm right. He wants this. In a way that renders him powerless.

With a shaking breath, I roll my shoulders back, thrusting my breasts up, letting the robe fall down just slightly. Then I part my thighs before I can talk myself out of it. His gaze lowers, the expression on his face one of hunger.

He unbuckles his belt, undoes his pants and frees himself, standing stiff and tall against his stomach. He curves his hand around his manhood, and begins to stroke himself. I lick my lips, and I reach out, wrapping my own hand around him. His breath hisses through his teeth, and he claps his hand over mine.

"Careful," he growls.

I stroke him, from base to tip, reveling in the feel of him. And how it makes me feel to touch him like this. Powerful and like the sort of goddess I have never fancied myself to be.

I've never thought about the foods that I liked. I've never thought about feeling beautiful. I've never thought about desire.

And now I feel like I'm satiating myself on it. Like I'm a glutton for these things that feel so good. These things that I've ignored entirely out of fear that I could never really have them.

It's a frightening, out-of-control feeling, but at least, holding him in my hand like this, I know that he is out of control too.

He reaches around me, lifts me up out of my chair and draws me onto his lap, kissing me, lowering his head and taking one of my breasts into his mouth. He sucks my nipple in deep, until the pleasure is so great that I have to cry out.

I feel my power slipping away, but it's such a glorious surrender. He turns me into this creature of overwhelming need, and I welcome it. All the resistance from a moment before is gone. He lifts his hand, pinches my nipple hard, the pleasure-pain combination brutal and glorious.

In the candlelight, he is fearsome. I put my hand on

his bare chest, run my fingers down the dips and hollows on his body. His muscles. His scars. It is a privilege to be so close to a man like him. One who is so terrifying to everyone else. But when he came apart before, he trembled. Inside of me.

I cup his face, and I kiss him. On the smooth side of his face, and then I move to kiss his scars. He groans beneath my mouth. I kiss down his neck, learning the texture of those scars. He moves his hands down my back, down to my hips, lifts me up and positions me over his cock, lowering me slowly, so that I can take him inch by inch, into my tender body. I'm sore, but it's more than worth it. He grips the back of my head, fingers pushed through my hair, and he closes his fist as he seats me on him completely, tugging hard as he thrusts up inside me.

And then I'm lost. In the primal nature of it. The rhythm of it.

The glow of the candles, the feel of him, the sounds that he makes. The sounds that I make. Whatever I was before, whoever I was before, maybe I'm simply not her now. I told him that a man didn't have the power to change a woman with sex. But my head is swimming, and I think that I might've been wrong about everything.

Because how has he done this to me? How has he taken me—sensible, cerebral—and turned me into a creature made entirely of my own desire?

I would beg him for anything. There's not a single thing he could ask of me, demand of my body, that I would find distasteful, not in this moment. Everything feels more than reasonable. It feels desirable. It feels wonderful. When he leans in and kisses me, then bites my neck, and soothes the sting away with his tongue, licking me, I only want more. He cups my face, his forehead pressed against mine as he thrusts up within me, growling each and every time. His fingers digging into me as he roars his completion, sending me over the edge into my own pleasure spiral. We hold each other. Breathing hard. I forgot that we were in the dining room. I forgot that anyone could walk in.

I forgot everything. Even my own name.

But I didn't forget his.

"Come," he says. "Let us go to bed, my queen."

He takes me naked from the room, and if there were any staff lingering, they dissipate. As though they sense that the king needs privacy. I find myself deeply unconcerned with the logistics of it. Especially when he takes me back to his room, lays me down in the center of the bed and tucks us both beneath the covers. When he strokes my face and kisses me lightly on the forehead as I begin to lose consciousness.

King Lucian, the Sea Serpent of the Mediterranean, the dragon in the cave, is my husband now.

I'm his prisoner.

I'm his wife.

Both of those things are true. Both of them are heavy.

But even holding them there at the center of my chest, I fall asleep in his arms.

CHAPTER TEN

I SPEND DAYS without a single thought in my head. It's strange, uncomfortable, and at the same time, it's like having a vacation from myself and the burdens that I've carried my entire life.

I'm not thinking about the future. I'm not thinking about what's right or wrong or good for me. What might be bad for me. I'm just in a state of surrender.

To his pleasure. To him.

I've spent my life learning. But I've never learned another human being. I'm learning Lucian. His moods, his expressions. The shift of every muscle, the particular way he sounds when he feels pleasure. At the same time, I'm learning something about myself.

I've surrendered to the experience. To what it means to feel. Only.

That night, our wedding night, when I fell asleep in his bed, I didn't make the conscious decision to put away my concerns and suspicions. I didn't decide to set it all aside and surrender. I just did. I woke up in his arms the next morning, and he claimed me, again and again. I spent that whole day in his bed.

Since then, we've done other things. He has a country to manage, and true to his word, he set me up with some online classes—they haven't started yet, thus my reprieve on thought—and I've also been presented with some charities that I might throw my weight behind.

But mostly, this has been a honeymoon, even if it is inside a castle.

I'm almost embarrassed how eager I am to see him every day. But really marinating in that embarrassment would require thought, and I'm not doing that. Instead, I'm lying naked on the foot of my bed in a sunbeam. I'm reading a science book. I don't consider that thought, because it isn't planning or anything to do with myself. It's just being in the moment. But I'm waiting for him.

So when I hear footsteps outside my door, I'm already setting the book aside when he opens it.

He sees me, and his eyes glow. The way that he wants me fills me with a kind of delight that I've never experienced before. I feel important in a way that I never have. It's such a strange thing. To feel like sexuality is powerful, like my body matters, when honestly I've always felt like a brain floating in a skull jar. Not anymore. I'm very much connected to every part of myself now. He's stripping his own clothes off before I can greet him, and he's taken me to ecstasy before we exchanged two words.

And yet, as he finds his own pleasure, pours himself inside of me, I feel like the look in his eyes speaks to feelings and truths that words wouldn't be sufficient for.

I feel like I'm perilously close to understanding

something I thought I didn't need to. The way that my sister falls so passionately into these kinds of relationships doesn't seem like a mystery to me anymore. She and my mother no longer feel like alien creatures that I can't understand.

Because before Lucian touched me, I didn't understand, and that version of myself would look at this version of myself and find her to be sad and woefully misguided. While I look back at the version of myself who didn't know this and I feel…she didn't know.

There was so much she didn't know.

It frightens more now than it did before, but I also understand why people decide to embrace it, terrifying and powerful though it is.

Which is part of why it compounds my fear.

"What do you have to do today?" I ask, my fingers tracing patterns on his chest.

"I'm finished for the day with everything but this," he says.

He takes hold of my hand and lifts it, kissing my palm. Then he picks me up from the bed, along with a bundle of blankets, and moves us down to a sunny patch on the floor that's big enough for the two of us. It's right in front of the bookshelves, and it's a cozy nook, but funny, because we could just stay on the bed. But I enjoy the strange things that he does. The ways in which he's oddly romantic. I wouldn't have ever said that I was a romantic person.

Maybe that's why I like his version of it. It's not hearts and flowers. It's midnight feasts and nests of blankets. It's endless orgasms and the way that he studies me like I'm a fascination.

"Have you read any of the novels that I've given you?"

"No," I say.

The look he gives me is stern and it does something to me. Makes my insides feel like they're melting. Makes my stomach drop. I curl into him, and he puts his arm around me. "Shall I read to you?"

"You want to…to read to me?"

"If it's the only way I'm going to get you to discover the merits of fiction…"

That is how we spend the afternoon. Lying on the floor in blankets as he reads *The Secret Garden*. It's a children's book. But it makes me cry. I watch his face as he reads, and I wonder what speaks to this man about that book. I wonder how it reaches him.

What it meant to him when he was a boy, and what it means to him now.

He looks up from the book, eyes connecting with mine. "What?"

"Which one are you?"

A crease appears between his brows as he considers this, and I can't help but marvel at the hard-cut lines of his face. I see his scars differently now. They shocked me at first, and while they never detracted from his beauty they added to his beastliness.

Now I see them as part of him.

"Are you the girl who came to live there, the one who discovered the secret garden, or are you the boy?" I press.

He considers this for a moment, his large hands cradling the book, an expression on his face that's almost…soft. Almost.

"Both," he says. "I spent my childhood in a certain amount of isolation. My imagination was an important part of my survival. But then, I've also been shut in. Lying in bed, trying to heal."

"But you didn't have a friend to come and draw you back out?"

He shakes his head. "No. And my parents were dead, so that meant that I was king."

"How old were you?"

I'm hungry for his story.

I know that it's printed in history books and the like. I know the dates, but somehow, looking at him, really taking in the reality of it, I need to personalize it more.

I need to hear it from him. His feelings on what happened, the facts beyond what the press printed.

"I was thirteen when I officially became king. There were advisors who handled things for the six months prior to that, the press, official statements. I was too injured to do much of anything."

"Lucian…"

"It's all right. It was a long time ago."

"But it hasn't faded." I lift my hand and touch his scars.

"It has," he says, taking hold of my hand and lowering it. "What you see, that is nothing in comparison to how it was."

"What were your parents like? I don't mean as king and queen. I mean as parents."

He makes a low noise in the back of his throat and looks up at the ceiling. "Busy. I loved them very much. My mother was exquisitely beautiful. My father tall and strong. I wanted to be like him. They had grand parties. And I remember watching them from the balcony in the ballroom. Gazing down at all of the opulence. Then the wars started and they closed the palace. My mother grew fearful. She stopped dressing up. My father became short-tempered. I understand, of course. The toll that it took on him. And truthfully, their anxieties were not misplaced. I was taken from the palace. By someone that they trusted. Held captive, tortured. I'm the reason my parents are dead, you see. Because they did try to rescue me. And when they did, it left them vulnerable to attack. It was demanded that they both appear to come and claim me."

"But they let you go?"

He laughs. "No. My father was not a fool. When he went that day, he had men lying in wait. Unfortunately, they could not save my parents. But they did save me."

Imagining him as a boy, one who had been hurt like that, then lost his parents, wounds me. But I know he doesn't want me to weep over him. He's telling me this with grave matter-of-factness. And I know that he won't welcome me being overly soft about it. So I just try to listen.

"That was actually what ended the war. The death of the king and queen. Other nations intervened at that point. They squashed the rebellion."

He takes a breath. "The very sad thing is I understand what the rebellion wanted. I've tried to give some of those things to the people. More freedom. More resources, though based on what you have said I still fall short. However, I cannot feel entirely sympathetic to their cause. As you must understand."

I nod. "I understand."

"Books were my only friends," he says. "And something of a guilty pleasure. Particularly after I became king. They didn't want me reading stories. They wanted me reading up on world events. On diplomacy. But I was still a boy. In many ways. Surrounded by adults. Responsibility."

The picture he paints is so poignant, almost especially so because of how evenly he tells it all. Like this is another story he's reading to me, not painful memories from his past.

"How did…how did your myth start?"

He lifts a brow. "My myth?"

"Yes, you know. Everything people say about you. That you're the Sea Serpent of the Mediterranean. The dragon of the castle on the rock, half monster, half man, all mad."

"Hmm." The sound is somewhere between a hum and a growl. "When I wouldn't make appearances, it started. They were right too. It was because I was disfigured. Because I had fits and rages and mercurial moods. If I'm honest, I was half mad after my parents died. After my torture."

"Why did you let it continue?" I ask, my chest aching. "Why did you…cultivate it?"

He rubs his chin, as if he's seriously considering it. "It suited me. I wanted to be frightening. I wanted to be someone who gave enough to the people that they would be happy, but also someone who would be seen as invulnerable." He pauses for a long moment. "Do you know, the worst thing about torture, it's not the pain. It's the lack of control. I wanted to be strong. I wanted to be strong enough that the videos they sent my family wouldn't compel them to risk themselves. I wanted to be strong. But I begged for my life." He takes a sharp breath. "I begged for my life. I cried when they burned me. When they cut me."

I want to kill them all. A rage I've never felt before floods my veins. I wasn't alive when this happened, I'll never meet the men who did it, likely long dead, but I want to raise them from the grave to destroy them.

How could they do this to him?

Lucian.

"You were a boy," I say, my heart feeling like it's about to crack. "You were just a boy."

"I was never really a boy. I was always meant to be a king. And when you are meant to be a king you have to be something different. You have to be something mythic. Something strong. I failed at that. It is my fault my parents are dead."

"No, it isn't," I say. "Any parent would rescue their child. Any good parent. It doesn't matter if you cried or not. Begged or not, they would've come for you."

"Regardless, it has never been a desire of mine to be reduced to that state ever again. That lack of control. That sniveling… No. I have fashioned for myself a reputation for being strong. As for the planes? That's how many of the rebels were sneaked into the country.

So many of them came from outside. And so, I have shut down flights to the country. You have to come through the port. Because I…"

It's trauma. I can see it. But I know that he won't characterize it that way. This iron fist that he's cultivated is something that he needs to make himself feel safe.

To make the country feel safe.

But he was taken out of this palace as a young boy, and he has to continue to live here. To rule here. The scars that came from what happened are on his skin. Every day. A reminder of everything he's been through. Maybe they have gotten better over time. Maybe it has gotten less painful. But it isn't gone.

He would rather be the dragon than ever be that boy again. And I understand that. I also ache for him. Because he's a man alone. A man kept so solitary. By his own rules and his position, by the pain that he's experienced. By the walls that he's built to protect himself.

But then he's also…this. Whatever he is to me. I'm not sure why he's so gentle with me, though even that is a bit of a contradiction. Because I'm his prisoner. But he's given his prisoner an awful lot of blankets.

I'm his prisoner that he reads to.

That he kisses as if I am special. Yes, it would be easy for me to think of it as him using me. Using my body for his own pleasure, but he doesn't. He shares pleasure with me. It doesn't feel like that. It doesn't feel like I am an object. He makes me feel beautiful.

He makes me feel desired.

I want to ask him more. About his marriages. About

what actually happened. But I can feel the walls around him. For a moment there, he opened the gate to me. He let me ask questions, but I can feel that they will close the moment he feels like I'm pushing him too much. I can't take advantage and ask everything all at once.

"What a terrible thing to lose your parents," I say. "My mother is one of the most important people in my life. If I would've lost her when I was twelve I think it would've changed me too."

"What happened to your father?"

I shake my head. "I've never known him. One of the men that my mother fell in love with over the years. But like most of them, he didn't stay. She's a romantic, though. She always believes that this one will be the one. I admire that in her. I know that some people resent their mothers for having a lot of relationships. I don't. She does a good job keeping it separate from her children. She always did. But she hopes. Time and time again. I've never been like that."

"And your sister?"

I shake my head. "Eve is a romantic. I told you, that's why I'm here. She's in love with Marcus, she wants to marry him. The idea of marrying you instead… It broke her."

"What about you?" His eyes are fierce.

"I didn't ever want to fall in love." I look away from him. "So I figured I wasn't going to lose anything by marrying a stranger."

"You wanted to go to school."

I nod. "Yes. But I weighed the consequences. I had

some hope that perhaps I could still… But they were silly hopes. I made my decision."

He makes that growling sound in his throat again. "Yes. You did. At twenty-two."

"And you were king at thirteen."

"I didn't have a choice."

"Neither did I."

"Meaning?"

I shake my head. "My sister's unhappiness was unbearable to me. And as long as I could do something about it, I was going to."

"Why?" He is completely baffled by this. And I wish that I had a better way to articulate it to him. Because I don't feel like what I did was entirely selfless. Particularly not now as I lie there with him. But I don't want to open up my chest and share the vulnerable feelings that have been growing inside of me for the past week. I don't want to start talking about things that I haven't even begun to make sense of.

I do want to share with him—he's done so with me, and generously.

But he is a man with twenty years more living than I've done. There are parts of myself that are unexplored. I thought it meant they didn't matter. That they weren't driving me. I think now that I'm wrong. I think there's more to me, to the reason I did this than I can easily untangle.

"It was a chance to do something big," I say. "I've had plans all of my life, to do something to get out of the life that we have here. Not that it's a bad life. We aren't destitute, even though we certainly don't have anything extra. But it isn't enough to truly change anything. To travel, to go to a university out of the country. To…to dream. It's a strange thing, because in some ways my mother and sister dream bigger than I ever have. You can't control someone else's heart. The audacity to believe that you can love someone at the same time they love you, and that it will continue on forever… That's bravery. You can't control that. You can't plan for it. I chose things that I could plan. But every year I fell short. Every year I couldn't quite get there because there was something else we needed money for. And I know that you're looking at me, and considering twenty-two very young, but for what I want to do time is passing me by."

I find a deeper part of myself, a deeper honesty than I've had before. I wasn't being entirely self-sacrificial. I was stuck. I didn't want to be. I have a sudden, clear insight into that. "And part of me just thought…to hell with it. At least this is big. And who knows where it will take me. I know where all of my planning will take me. Up each and every slow, incremental step. But I was tired of taking steps. I wondered what it would be like if I could fly."

It seems foolish now, because of course being a queen gives you power, resources, money, but it doesn't give you a normal life. It has given me something different, but it is something with a lot more weight than I imagined. A testament, yet again, to the things that I failed to give importance to.

Certainly, somewhere in there, is the humanity of Lucian himself.

He was a symbol to me when I arrived. A legend. He is a man to me now, though I can't say that means I have him figured out.

"And then I clipped your wings," he says, looking at me with something like sorrow in those blue eyes.

"But your story makes me understand something," I say. "Your wings are clipped too. You're bound to this life. To all the things you have to do. Heavy is the head that wears the crown."

I roll onto my back and stare up at the ceiling. "My grandmother got abandoned by my grandfather. My mother was abandoned by my father. By Eve's father. I worry that Eve will also be abandoned. All of these things made me afraid to dream in many ways. Planning, yes. Dreaming, no. Maybe that's why I've never liked fiction. Because it feels like a dream."

He shifts, looms over me, brushes his knuckles against my cheek. "Will you dream of me, sparrow?"

What else is a caged sparrow with clipped wings to dream of? But I don't ask him that.

Instead, I kiss him. I kiss him with every ounce of desire that is in me. Not just the desire that I feel for him, but this reckless, endless desire that I have for my own life. This need to soar. To succeed. To do something and be something. This impossible paradox, that now I've become a queen, but won't recognize my dreams. That now I am more important to the world in some ways, but my own life has become smaller and smaller.

Smaller.

But…

He lifts his head and looks at me, and I grip his face and kiss him, push him onto his back and climb over top of him. I sit astride him, looking down at all his masculine glory. As he allows me this power. As he allows me to assume this position, this role. That's what it will always be. What he allows. Because he could push me off at any moment. He could claim the dominant position. He is allowing me to feel powerful. Can I accept that? Can I accept a life where everything is what he allows?

I don't know what other option I have. Not now.

His hands span my waist; he moves them up my body, thumbs grazing over my nipples. For all that he has made my life smaller, he has made it so much bigger too, and that is another thing that's hard for me to reconcile.

Without Lucian, I would never have felt my body like this. I would never have realized how much this part of me mattered. I had locked this part of myself away. I was so afraid.

I already want so much. I would never have been able to bear life if I wanted more. If I wanted a man to look at me and think that I was beautiful. If I wanted to be touched, kissed, held. If I wanted to be someone's wife.

It was out of reach enough to want to make it to university. I could never have borne the weight of more dreams.

They are dreams. Whatever I've spent all these years telling myself. I'm a dreamer. I just didn't want to be.

Suddenly, I'm overcome by the weight of those desires. Of everything that I want.

Everything that I can't have. No one can have everything, I suppose. This man, this king, has been denied so many things. Tortured, isolated. How long has it been since someone has loved him?

The question terrifies me so I push it away. Shut it down deep. I don't want the answer to that question. I don't. I don't want to be confronted by it.

I don't want to have to think about it.

Thinking is the enemy right now. Why can't I just keep on feeling? God, but the feelings are overwhelming. They're expanding in my chest, moving all through my body. I want him. I maneuver my hips, arch them back so that I can take him inside me. It's not close enough. I want him, and it's driving me. Tearing me to pieces. I want more, and I don't know what to call that. I want more from everything. For myself, from him, from the world.

I feel like I'm being remade into something new, and it is painful. Unimaginable. And yet it's also beautiful and wonderful and the most glorious thing I've ever experienced.

Lucian is unlike anyone I've ever known. Awakening things in me that are strange and wonderful and brilliant.

He has shown me the power in feeling.

But that is a double-edged sword. Like everything else with him.

I ride him until I cry out. Until he grips my hair and

flips me over onto my back, drives us both into oblivion. Then kisses me like I'm made of glass.

He has taken things for me. He has given things to me. He has made my life smaller and larger.

And I'm left wondering what I've done to change his.

CHAPTER ELEVEN

It goes on like this. The way that we want each other is almost like torture. The passage of time does nothing to stop it. If he's with me, he's inside me, which is why it's an incredible shock when I start bleeding. My cramps are terrible, and I can't get out of bed. I would've thought that a man working so hard to produce an heir would surely be rewarded with one. Particularly because it seems like even biology wouldn't dare defy Lucian.

But mine has.

For the first time, a strange new fear winds through me. He chose me to be his bride—well, he allowed me to trade places with my sister—and we never established whether or not I was actually fertile. There are options, I know that, but I don't know what he considers to be an option.

And yet again, I'm left with the wrenching push and pull of my own desires. In some ways I'm relieved that I'm not pregnant. I can't imagine being a mother in nine months' time. I can't imagine being a mother. It just wasn't part of my plans, and it's going to take some time for me to wrap my head around the fact that my whole future is going to be different. Knowing it, and truly being able to imagine it, to accept it, are different things. But I also feel strangely sad. Worried. Anxious. That could also be my hormones.

My PMS tends to take the form of anxiety. It chews at me, makes me want to plan things, set things into motion, something to protect me from the relentless crush of time, and all of the things that I can't control.

I take breakfast and lunch in bed, and by the afternoon, Lucian comes for me. "Are you quite well?"

I can see the tension on his face. Is he hoping that I have morning sickness?

I'll spare him the anticipation.

"I'm not pregnant," I say. "I'm on my period. My cramps are particularly vile today is all."

Except that's not all. Because how could it be? He doesn't say anything; he disappears from the room. Of course. I'm no use to him as long as I'm bleeding. He can't even get satisfaction, and I'm not carrying his baby.

What a useless wife.

My thoughts are such a dark, grumpy cloud, and unfair besides. He didn't say any of that.

But I'm in a terrible mood. When he reappears with a tray containing two large pieces of cake—one strawberry, one chocolate—a heating pad tucked underneath his arm, I don't even know what to say.

He sets the cake on the bed beside me, drags a chair to the side of the bed and places the heating pad on my stomach. I look at him, lower it just slightly to where I need it. "That… Thank you."

"Have you not realized by now that I'm not a monster?"

He has been content to let everyone else think so. But never me.

Not from the first, and I don't understand why.

I can't speak, because I'm afraid I'll cry, which is a horror I don't even know how to cope with, because I'm not a crier. Though, I've cried more times since coming to this palace than at any other time in recent memory. Twice. Which still isn't a lot, but is notable.

"I know you aren't," I say.

"You're upset," he says.

"Yes. I am upset."

"Why? Is it something that I did?"

"It's everything," I say, ready to lash out. Ready to be mean because everything inside of me feels jagged. "I'm not pregnant. And thank God. Because I'm too young to have a baby. But here I am, married to you, expected to have a baby. We never had protected sex, and we have sex all the time. I think that we have sex more than anybody in the whole world. It might actually be a problem."

His expression remains measured. "Do you find my attentions unwanted?"

I shake my head. "No. Ours is a mutual sickness."

I can't lie to him about that.

"I see. You are…infected as I am?"

"*Yes*," I say. There's a lump in my throat, and I'm furious. "But having a baby would really mean giving up on all my dreams."

"I can see how that would be."

"You've taken all my dreams anyway," I say.

He says nothing, his jaw tenses, his mouth flat.

"What if I can't get pregnant, Lucian?" Because perversely, that is my other deep and terrible fear. Because then he might get rid of me. He's already had three wives. Why not four? What if he has taken me, shown me all of this, upended my life, and he'll just put me back out if I can't produce his heir?

Then you'll go on like it never happened. That won't be so bad. It won't be. You have had this time where you learned all about sex, and experienced living in a castle, and then you could just...go on.

I want him to say something, and he doesn't. He doesn't leave either. He sits there with me, saying nothing. His expression grave.

He leaves eventually, and returns with a fresh heating pad later. I'm served dinner in the room after that.

He doesn't come and visit me over the next couple of days, and I'm furious. Even though what he did was kind, I've decided to internalize being angry that he was more distant when he couldn't have sex with me because it does something to feed my insecurities. My hormones are monstrous and I want to embrace it.

After five days of that, I have some clarity. My hormone fog has cleared slightly, and I don't feel as unreasonable. It's also interesting, because the reprieve of sex, not being around him, has made me feel a little bit more like myself too.

The feelings inside of me are unfamiliar. But I am still me. Going back to reading textbooks, to reading new studies, that makes me feel a little bit more centered. Just because I'm not going to school doesn't mean I can keep learning. I have my classes that I'll be starting soon online. I don't have everything, and I want everything, and that's difficult. So much for being practical, I suppose.

I'm just not.

With some trepidation, I go down after dinner and move into the library, where I know I'll find Lucian.

I'm not disappointed.

"Good evening," he says, looking up at me.

"I'm not bleeding anymore," I say.

"Glad to hear it. Is it always particularly tough on you?"

"I admit I do get quite emotional. Though I think there were some contributing factors."

"I can see that," he says.

I'm annoyed, because I think he sounds a little bit amused, and nothing was funny about the way that I felt.

He smiles, and I'm enraged. "Do not look at me that way," he says. "Sit down."

I do, but seriously.

"Why are you angry with me?"

"Because I… I don't know."

"You are upset. About the strictures of royal life. About…the heir."

"Yes," I say.

"I want you to get on the pill."

I jolt. "What?"

"You're not ready to have a child."

"But that's part of the deal."

"It was. When I was choosing a wife. And not you. You are not ready to have a child. You were obviously very unhappy about it, and the fallout of the emotions over you finding out that you weren't pregnant were very intense."

It wasn't that simple, but I decide to allow him that. "Yes," I say.

"We can wait. One of the deeply unfair things about life and biology—and I should not have to tell you about biology—is that men can have babies for a much longer period of time than women can. You're young. You can afford to wait. I'm not young, but I can certainly wait."

"But—"

"And now you argue with me. When I offer you what you want." He sounds baffled.

"I… I don't know what to do with you. Because sometimes you make all these commands, and tell me how things are going to be, and even when it's you giving me what you think I want, you're not asking me."

He's silent, and looks chastised. Which is about as shocking as anything could be. "Would you like to go on the pill?"

It will be a reprieve for some of my worries. It will give me time to adjust to my life. And will give us more time as a couple. A couple? Is that what we are? Obviously. Except…it isn't like that really. We aren't bonded by romance. By love. He does things that are romantic. He is my lover. And yet couples bring to mind something domestic; we aren't that. But we are two people trying to figure out how to live with one another, I suppose. Which really isn't something I thought would happen with him.

"I'm sorry," I say. "If I'm being honest with you, I imagined that you would be my adversary. That I would hate you. That you would take your husbandly rights, and leave me. I didn't imagine that you would talk to me. Or buy me books." I didn't imagine he would be so complicated. Controlling and giving, rigid, but caring. It would've been easier if he hadn't engaged my emotions. But he has. That's the difficult piece. If he had only ever remained a figure, something I was fighting against, then all of this would be much easier. I could resist him, and not all of these things in myself.

"I'm sorry that I fall short," he says.

"I would like to go on the pill," I say. I press my hands against my forehead. "Thank you for giving me a choice."

He nods slowly. "I have been thinking. I have to go on a diplomatic trip. To Europe. I'm wondering if you would like to come with me."

"You said that I was never going to leave the palace."

He nods again. "I did say that. But you're unhappy."

That he's concerned about my lack of happiness is astonishing to me. I would not have thought that it would matter to him at all. "I have no investment in your misery," he says. "But you…you have heard my story. My reason for not allowing flights into the country other than my own."

"You're afraid," I say.

"With good reason. I don't want for anything to happen to you."

It's such a strange admission, because there is no current danger, but he's projected his anxiety onto me. Knowing that he cares in some capacity about me personally. But of course he does. Because I know him well enough to know he isn't controlling for the sake of it. He's not a cruel man. Nothing that he's done would ever lead me to believe he was.

"I know you might find this difficult to believe, but I lived in the world for all of these years without you."

"But you weren't tied to me." His voice is rough. "I don't have the best outcomes with people who join themselves to me."

Yet again, I want to ask about his other wives. But I find that something is stopping me. That there are some things I don't really want to know. Even though part of me is curious.

"But you're letting me out of my cage," I say. It feels like something. Maybe like progress.

"I am bringing your cage with me," he says.

I don't know if he's being serious, if he's teasing me, or if he's reminding me of exactly who he is. That no matter he might make concessions, I belong to him.

He's right. I surrendered to this. For him. Now all I can do is be grateful that he's doing this at all.

I've never been on a plane. It's…terrifying, actually. Even though I know this is luxury travel, we are hurtling through the air at an alarming rate of speed. I am aware the speed is a feature and not a bug. But even so, I find it unnerving. The flight to France isn't a long one but I'm restless all the same.

"I assumed you'd traveled," he says.

"You make it very difficult."

"I don't intentionally make it difficult to travel," he says. "I just try to keep the airspace on the island clear."

"Which means that your citizens first have to take a boat somewhere else if they want to fly. We've never had that kind of money. And I've been…saving. You already know that."

"Yes," he says. "I do. But I confess that I assumed you had been to some of these universities that you were dreaming about going to."

"No," I say. "I just looked at them online."

He appears discomfited by this, and I can't figure out why. I can't figure out why he cares, since part of our relationship is him limiting my access to things. But he also likes giving me things. Maybe he feels the push and pull the same way that I do.

He is bringing me on this trip. And I might feel pleased about that once the plane actually lands.

I'm right. When the plane descends in Paris, and I see the overhead view of this city that I've seen depicted so many times on TV, in movies and books, I forget everything. If the plane were to go down right now, I might not even be that sad.

We are ushered from the aircraft and into a luxury car, and my face is glued to the window as we drive through the city streets. As I take in the glory of the architecture.

"You are so strange," he says.

I rip my gaze away from the view and stare at him. "I'm strange?"

"Yes. You, who claim to have no dreams. Who claim you have no interest in fiction. This little scientist. You're the most sensual woman I've ever known. You love beautiful things. You love to be touched." We have a driver, and no partition up between us, and I shift uncomfortably as he describes me—accurately—with an audience.

"You love food, even though you decline to tell me your favorite. You yearn for adventure, but are afraid of air travel."

"I just hadn't done it before," I say, sniffing.

"You are not practical, Queen Lilith. You are greedy. Insatiable. You don't just want one thing, you want it all. I am uncertain why you can't admit it."

"Because I can't have it all," I say. "I already told you. Watching my mother and sister made me afraid to dream. And anyway, I'm not wrong. I'm the queen now. I still can't have everything."

He considers this. "No. None of us can."

"I never wanted to live with that unbearable ache."

"To live, I suspect, is to have an unbearable ache. The world is vast, and there are so many experiences. None of us can have all of them." He's now looking out the window. "I suspect there is some beauty in that. Knowing that the world contains so much glory, and we cannot experience all of it. It is compensation for all the sadness the world contains."

"It's another sadness," I say. "If you want too much."

"I suppose that's one way of viewing it," he says.

I wonder if the reason he sees it this way is because of how much more time he's lived. It makes me feel like there's a cavern standing between us. I don't know why I care about that at all.

The car pulls up to a luxury estate with wrought iron gates, glorious and vast. "This is the chancellor's lodgings. We will be starting here, and stay for a couple of days. We can do some sightseeing, and then we will move on to England."

"Oh," I say. Because I can't help myself. I've always wanted to go there. I want to see Oxford. I've always wanted that. It's where I wanted to go. Me and so many other people. But it makes me feel like if I could do it I would be…

That I would matter.

Maybe walking through the halls would be enough.

"What?"

"I've always wanted to go there. I mean, not just to visit, it's where I wanted to go. I… I had a tentative acceptance. Because of the focus of my research."

"And what is that?"

"Cancer cells," I say. "The way that they grow."

"I see. Why medical research?"

"Because it matters," I say.

"And you want to matter."

I look at him. "How? The idea that I could do something significant for the world, even being a person who is often so insignificant in every way. I suppose that's why my mother and sister look for love. Romantic love, I mean. That's where they get that feeling from. That they matter."

"But you don't."

I shake my head. "That's depending on another person a bit too much for me."

Ironic. Especially considering the image that he left me with before we arrived here. That he's carrying my cage.

But at least he's carried it somewhere nice.

We're sharing a room in the estate, and practically we often do, but we have our own separate quarters that we can go to otherwise, so this is interesting. A shared space for several days. He has diplomacy during the day, and I am allowed to see the city with security detail. I go to the Louvre, and I find peace in art in a way that I never thought I would.

It makes me think about what he said about me. About how I am a dreamer. How I want *everything.*

But I don't have everything. He's not even here with me in the museum and I find that sad. But that night we dress up and go to a dinner with the diplomat, his wife and a few other key political people. The person I'm most interested in is Dr. Isabel Swift, who I'm starstruck to meet, honestly. She's a pioneer in the field of infectious disease research and even though that isn't my focus, I've read a lot of her work.

"I just finished reviewing the Stanford Study," I tell her as I take a sip of the finest wine I've ever had in my life. For a moment I feel like I do have everything.

She looks surprised. "You read medical studies for fun? I didn't expect to meet anyone here who knew what I did at all."

"Oh, I'm… Well, I was studying to go to school to

do medical research but obviously I…can't do that now. I can still have an education just not the way I wanted."

"Why can't you?" she asks.

"I married a king," I say. "Which as far as furthering career goals goes is a bad move."

"What did you want to do?"

I download all of my aspirations onto her, but I'm careful about what I say in regards to my marriage because even if it's strange, I feel protective of Lucian, and what we have.

"Do you want a university tour? Because I can arrange for you to have one—not that your husband can't, given that he's a king, but I have contacts in the research department—"

"Yes!" The very idea of getting a tour at Oxford has me so excited I don't even try to play it cool.

I'm so excited about my conversation with Dr. Swift that my enthusiasm carries over to dinner, and I fear I'm much more talkative than I would normally be. I'm not suffering from the comparison terror, or any of the awkwardness I felt back at the wedding. I'm not really sure why. But there's something about sitting next to Lucian, who looks at me with approval, that adds to my confidence.

"Your wife is a gem," says the diplomat. It is a sincerely given compliment, and though he's speaking to my husband and not to me, I receive it. "You should do everything you can to hang onto this one."

I'm reminded that if Lucian has been here before, then these men have met his previous wives. They've seen a side of him not even his own country ever sees.

They're all even older than he is, and they would have known…

That dims some of my light. After dessert, we're mingling about in the study, and Isabel comes to sit beside me. "Are you okay?"

"I'm fine," I say.

"What did he mean by that? 'Hang onto this one.'"

"I'm rather famously Lucian's third wife," I say. I look down at my hands. "It seems foolish, doesn't it? His third wife, in her twenties, with the others long gone. We must actually look quite like a joke."

Isabel frowns. "No. You don't at all. He seems like he cares about you very much."

On his own terms, I suppose he does. Maybe. But what is care to Lucian? I think back on his childhood. On how desolate it was. Has he really ever had any kind of care? And if so, does he really know how to give it? He tries. But I'm like a pet to him, really. I get some nice little things, and he gets everything he wants.

I've been letting my feelings get too intense. In the palace it's easy to do. It's only us. Out here, I feel so much more tender. I feel young, I don't feel like his equal. I feel like a silly girl for believing he might feel deeply for me.

"He's kind," I say.

"You care about him. That comment hurt your feelings."

"I don't like to be reminded about… I don't even know anything about them."

"Well, that's understandable. But he's not… You don't think he's actually dangerous."

"He didn't kill his wives. I know that much." He may not have told me everything yet, but I do know he's not capable of true cruelty. I don't need him to tell me in order to know.

Isabel nods. "You seem like a very smart woman. I'm sure you know who you're married to."

I'm not sure about that. And I chew on that for the rest of the evening. But I don't turn Lucian away when he turns to me in bed.

I'm also relieved when it's time for us to go to England. I exchanged numbers with Isabel the night of the dinner, and she texts me before our plane lands, telling me that my tour is arranged.

"Lucian," I say, as we descend into London. "Isabel Swift has arranged for me to take a tour of the research facilities at Oxford. I can come anytime this week."

He looks up from his book. "If you wish."

"I do wish. Please. I know that… I know that I will never go to school. I understand that. But it's my dream to even be able to see a place like this."

"You enjoyed talking to her."

"Yes. She's a premier researcher in the field of infectious disease."

"I know that," he says. "I confess I just didn't realize how exciting that might be for you."

"Science captured my attention from the time I was a child. It contains truth, which I find comforting. But there's also so much left to be discovered. Both of those things together make it seem like magic. I want to be part of it. I want to be in the middle of it. Making magic. The kind that can give people answers, and save lives."

"I doubt I've ever been half so passionate about anything as you are about this," he says, his expression filled with wonder.

"Oh well… I know passion isn't especially mysterious or cool but I…"

"I've never cared about that either. It's only that my ability to love much of anything was taken from me a long time ago."

"I know," I say. A reminder to me that he isn't really my enemy. My feelings were hurt, and I let myself get wounded. There's no need to be like that; he hasn't done anything to me.

"Do you think that you might be able to do some of the sightseeing with me?"

"I will be busy doing negotiations. But I will at least try to do the Oxford tour with you."

"I would like that," I say.

That's when I decide that I'm going to arrange something nice for him as well.

The morning of the tour we take a private train car from London and even though it feels strange with all our security detail, that's when I spring my surprise on him. Our walking tour of the favorite haunts of C. S. Lewis and J.R.R. Tolkien.

He looks at me as if he's been hit in the head. "When did you plan this?"

"When we got here. I mean, to England. I did a little bit of research, and I colluded with the security guards to arrange for our travel to give us time."

"I like it," he says. "Very much. I can't remember the last time anyone ever gave me a gift. Particularly not one so thoughtful."

My eyes fill with tears. I examine his face, my dragon. I don't even really see the scars anymore. Or rather, I don't see them as separate from him. There isn't a perfect side of his face, and a ruined one. There is only Lucian.

We walk along a placid green, the smooth pond full of ducks creating a pastoral scene, particularly with the glory of Oxford in the distance. It's easy to imagine being a literary sort, wandering and letting ideas swirl around in my head. Though, I've never considered myself creative. I wonder if Lucian does. He loves books. I wonder if he would've tried to write one if his life were different.

I wonder who he might've been.

Seeing him like this makes me ache. I wish I could know this man. But then I wouldn't have the one I know already. Both possibilities make me so terribly sad. All of my feelings for him are just too big.

I hurt myself on him constantly. What he says, what he doesn't say, what others say. What I can't ask, what I won't ask. I've been dumped into a relationship—a marriage—with no previous experience with such a thing and sometimes I feel like I'm drowning.

But I don't want to let go of him either.

When we finish the tour, and arrive at the main research building, he stops me just before we enter the building. He puts his hand on my cheek. "Thank you, sparrow."

"You're welcome," I say, trying to dampen the smile rising on my face just slightly. Because I don't want to look overly pleased with myself.

But I am.

Because no one has given him gifts. But I have. Because I know him. Or at least, I'm starting to. But there's still so much to him… He is a cavernous vault. Containing a whole dragon hoard, I assume. Of years, experience, knowledge. He doesn't want me to access it. He doesn't want anyone to; it isn't personal. He's told me things, so many things, but I want more. I want all of him.

I don't even know what all of him is.

I wonder if he does.

I'm introduced to so many venerable experts of the field that I'm dizzy before we even begin to tour the facility. It's everything I could've ever imagined. Part of me breaks inside, imagining what it would've been like to live here. To study here. To talk to these people, every day, share information as we make new discoveries. To go out onto the quiet greens, to stare at that same pond that Tolkien did, not to think about a fantasy world, but think about our own. That isn't my life. It's not going to be.

I had a dream. And I have to let it go. Admitting those things to myself is difficult. I wanted it. Enough that it hurts. It's not going to happen. I don't want being here to be a sad thing. It's a dream of a kind to even get to stand here. It's something more than what I was going to get. And I just have to be grateful for the afternoon.

We don't travel back to London. Instead, we go to a country manor house, which has been beautifully outfitted for our use. As ever, with Lucian, there is a splendid feast for dinner, and I find myself trying to taste it, trying to enjoy it, as I reflect on the afternoon spent partway in a dream.

"Are you well?"

"Just sad," I say. "But thank you."

"Why are you sad?" He sounds genuinely concerned.

"Because it was a little window into a life I might've had. And I'm just trying to let it go. It's something that I wanted. It's something that I dreamed of for myself. It was wonderful. As wonderful as I thought it would be. Sometimes when you see something in real life it doesn't measure up. But this did. It was everything and more. Part of me is glad that a place like that exists. Something that's every bit as magical and brilliant as you think it might be. But part of me is sad. Because I have to let it go. You are right. I'm as much a romantic as anyone in my family. I just romanticize different things."

"You can't have it because of me," he says.

"That's right," I say, looking up at him.

"You know, you make a wonderful impression on everyone, everywhere we go."

"I appreciate that."

"You were upsct, that night in France, when the diplomat said that I needed to hang onto you."

I'm surprised that he noticed that.

"I was."

"Why?"

"Because I realize that almost everyone in that room knew something about you that I didn't. Not just people you live with in a palace, but these people across the world. And consequently, they know things about my marriage that I don't. They met your previous wives, didn't they?"

He's silent for a moment. "They met Colette. I don't think anyone ever met Andrea."

"Colette," I say. I test her name out. That was his first wife. I know her name; everyone does. She was princess of one of the other Mediterranean islands in the Sun Belt. Their wedding was supposed to be a celebration, a demonstration of unity, ushering in a new era. Instead, within two years she was dead, and many people blamed Lucian.

After all, there had long been rumors about his madness. His rages.

A beautiful queen, who never bore the king a child, dies in a country that verges on medieval, and people begin to suspect the medieval thing.

"We were very young when we got married," he says. "Younger even than you. I was twenty-one. She was nineteen."

"Oh," I say. He's silent. And I need to know, even if part of me doesn't want to know. "Did you love her?"

He doesn't answer immediately. It looks like he's in another time. Another place. Like he's searching for something. For answers, or a memory. "I thought I did," he says. "At the time. She was beautiful, and she was…" He looks as if he's weighing the words in his mouth. "She was my first woman. You do feel quite like you are in love after your first time when you're so young." He looks at me with no small amount of irony, and I want to slide under the table. I don't like how clearly he sees me. I also don't like how clearly I'm able to see him. And I feel…jealous.

Yes. That's what it is. Jealousy. Because at one time, there was a woman who had him, young and a little bit less hard, maybe. A version of him who was discovering desire, rather than wielding it expertly as he does with me.

A woman who had that sort of giddy feeling with him that I do sometimes. A feeling that I'm certainly alone with.

"I'm surprised," I say. "That there was no one before her."

He brushes his knuckles down the scarred side of his face. "There were reasons I didn't pursue sexual relationships. You know I was not well. Not just physically, but I had many concerns about the physical. When I knew I had to take a wife, I also knew I had to get over it." He laughed. "I did. I thought… I rather thought we were something like happy. For a while. We didn't need to talk about the past. I just tried to play the role of husband and she was my wife. She was very good. She…she liked people, more than I ever did."

"But she wasn't happy?"

He shakes his head. "No. Colette had quite a long struggle with depression. For most of her life, actually. Not just when she was married to me. But I… I didn't know." His gaze gets extremely distant. "When I found her body on the rocks below the tower window I was so sure someone had done it to her. That the palace had been breached again. That it was like when my parents and I were taken. I… Until I found her note. After that I began to learn more about her, the real her. All the things she wrote in her diaries but never told me. How sad she was, and had been for years, even back to her childhood. It overwhelmed her."

"Lucian," I say, my breath filled with my own grief. At the image of him finding his young wife. At this certainty that he'd felt that everything was all right, and then it wasn't.

"That night in the garden, when I couldn't find you, I was very worried that you might've harmed yourself. I have learned that I'm not good at identifying the signs of what someone else is actually feeling. I don't want you to be sad, sparrow. I'm trying to make you happy."

I blink, my eyes filling with tears. "Depression isn't as easy as happy or sad. It actually has to do with how your brain functions. That's not my area of study, but I've done quite a lot of reading about it. In many ways she might've been happy with you. As happy as she could've been. It's only that her brain might also have been making things feel so heavy. Unbearable. You know, you can see it on a brain scan. The way that some people can't produce serotonin and dopamine."

"I know," he says. "Still, I regret it all the same. All these years on."

What a horrible thing that I feel jealousy still. Over the deep emotion this man must carry for her twenty years later. I see it on his face. The pain. The regret.

It's ridiculous to be jealous. She's gone, and his emotions are still there, and that seems fair. A tribute to her in some ways, since she's not here anymore.

But I'm his wife, and I find that I feel tender over it.

"Why did you let people think…?"

"What am I going to say? In her culture what happened is seen as a disgrace. A weakness. We said that it was an accident, people didn't believe it. In order to clarify it, we would have to tell the truth, and that would change her story, and her legacy. It didn't seem fair. In many ways I felt like perhaps I did kill her. That life with me was the thing that made it too unbearable. I didn't think so, I thought we had enough happiness, enough love that the difficulty wasn't so terrible. I was wrong. If you think I'm difficult now, you should've seen me then."

Perversely, I'm jealous of that too. I want to know him. The version of him then, the version of him now. Every version of him always.

"What about Andrea?"

He laughs. "Not dead."

"What?"

Of all the revelations he might have given me, that wasn't what I expected.

"Andrea is not dead. We married, and we never consummated the union. It became clear to me quite quickly that it wasn't going to work."

"Why?"

"She's a lesbian."

"*Oh*," I say.

"Yes. Which she told me after we married, and also

told me that she would try to lie back and think of England, so to speak. I told her I wasn't interested in such a sacrifice. But there was no going back to her family—they would only have married her off to someone else. They never would have accepted her. They were…from another time. So we hatched a plan. We annulled the marriage in secret—the priest knows, it couldn't be helped, but as we never consummated that was easy enough. I helped her fake her death, she ran off to be with her lover, who she is now married to. She's living under a different name in America. Far away from her family. And far away from any prying eyes."

"So you…you took the blame for that as well?"

"It became part of my legend, did it not? And as I said to you before, it felt somewhat fitting. And beneficial. At the time, it seemed like a decent idea. All these years on it is ill-fitting. But then…"

"You're punishing yourself," I say. "Letting people think all these things about you."

"I don't know that I'm punishing myself," he says. "But I had no investment in my own reputation. Not when there are aspects of it I deserve."

"All you did was care for a woman who suffered from depression. All you did was help another woman going to live her life."

"Yes. I suppose so."

It's awful of me to be relieved that he didn't love Andrea. That they didn't even have an intimate relationship, though then I have follow-up questions about all the other women he might've been with. "Who do you sleep with?"

"You, sparrow."

"Before me."

He lets out a slow breath. "There are always women who want danger. I'm happy to oblige. I told you, my reputation suits me. And in many ways it's well-earned. Do not think that I am some kind of tragic figure, or a savior. The fact of the matter is, I have leaned into this for all these years. You would like to hear that I'm actually good and celibate, wouldn't you? I am so sorry. I cannot count how many women I've taken to bed. And I don't know their names. Nor do I care to learn them."

He's saying that to distance me. It's also true, though. I see it in the tortured lines of his face. What I also see is he's not proud of this. It isn't nothing to him. He doesn't like the man that he's become, and that is a stark, shocking revelation.

He's made the world hate him, but even more than that, he hates himself.

He is pushing me away here, and I'm not quite sure why. If his marriages really are a source of pain or if it's something else.

"Well, as long as everyone consented," I say, looking down at my dinner.

He laughs. "A funny thing coming from you."

"What's that?"

"Many would argue that *you* didn't consent."

"I did," I say. "And have a hundred times since."

"Our age gap is very problematic," he says. "And I am a king. You were forced into the marriage."

"I want you," I say.

"You didn't *choose* me."

"I don't know exactly what you want me to say. I didn't. I didn't choose you. I don't hate you. And you aren't…forcing me to do anything. Ever. When we have sex I actually feel like I understand you. Or something close to it."

"You should go to university."

Suddenly, his prickliness, his relentless pushing me away, makes some sense, but that's the only thing that makes sense.

"What?"

I'm shocked by what he's saying.

"You had a tentative acceptance anyway, didn't you?" he asks.

"Yes. I did. But—"

"I am absolutely certain that if I make a phone call you will be admitted to the university."

"I don't want *you* to get me admitted. I worked hard for this on my own."

"You cannot have everything," he says, his tone stern. Angry. "Please don't be unreasonable."

"I don't understand you," I say. "You told me that there was no way that I could do this. You told me that I couldn't go anywhere, and now we're in England, and then you told me that you were simply carrying me in a cage. So what is this, and what am I supposed to make of it?"

"I am trying to give you what you want, and you are being fucking ungrateful."

"I'm confused," I say. "Because you've made it clear that while you want me to have the things I want, you mainly want it your way. You don't care about what I want exactly."

"I care," he growls. "I don't want you to jump out a tower window, sparrow, because I've clipped your wings and you cannot fly."

The heavy regret in his voice stabs at me. Of course, he's afraid that I'm going to hurt myself. Especially after the conversation about Colette. And as much as I want to take him up on his offer, I'm also not going to manipulate him into it. Not with his feelings.

Or maybe, I simply don't want a gift that's actually something that belongs to another woman. A dead woman.

"I don't want to be a token that you're using to try and salve your guilt."

"I'm not," he says. "You are brilliant. I was listening to you talk to Dr. Swift. I don't understand half of what it is either of you said, but you are brilliant. And the world should have your brilliance. If I keep you in a cage, then all of your gifts stay in that cage with you. It is a disservice to you, and to everyone. You deserve better. Better than that. And I have changed my mind. I'm not going to keep you caged. I'm going to allow you to go to school. If that is still what you want."

The grief that I've been processing since we left Oxford crashes on me now in a wave. To think that this is right in front of me. That all I have to do is reach out and grab it…

"I will arrange it. You don't even have to return to the palace. I will have everything you need sent here."

"You would…you would really do that for me?"

"Yes," he says. "As I've said before, you are young. You are young, and why shouldn't you try to have as many of your dreams as you can?"

I stand up, and I move to him, thoughtless, wrapping my arms around his neck and sitting on his lap, burying my head in his neck. "You're really doing this for me."

"Don't," he says. "I am doing nothing for you except…getting out of your way."

He melts me with that, and I can't be angry, not anymore.

"Thank you," I say, lifting my head and looking at him. Then I lean in and kiss him. He picks me up, standing out of the chair, and carries me up to a bedroom. I'm not even sure that it's the one we are going to be staying in tonight. Though, I suppose now it is.

He's hungry, fiercely so, and he strips me of my clothes quickly, kissing my neck, all the way down my body. Normally he takes his time. Normally he makes sure I have at least one orgasm before he's inside of me. He doesn't do that tonight. He sheaths himself in a condom—he's been protecting me ever since we decided that I would start taking the pill, waiting for a long enough period to pass to ensure that it's working—and thrusts inside of me. I cling to him, trying to ride the wave of his ferocity. But I can't control it. All I can do is surrender to him.

His movements are so feral, so fierce, he pushes me up the mattress, my head hitting the headboard. The bed crashes against the wall, and I fear that we may have to pay for the damage caused by this union. But that I remember that I'm married to a king, and cracked plaster is not a concern.

"You want this," he says.

"Yes," I say. "I want you."

He grits his teeth, pressing his forehead against mine, and I lose my control. I cry out his name, and he breathes out mine, and then we hold each other after. Like it's the end of something.

"You will go to school," he says. "Because it's what you wanted. It's what you wanted before you were forced into this. Because you have to."

"What happened to me taking classes online?"

"It's never going to be the same. It's never going to be your dream. You won't be in a room with all of these people who share your passion. You won't be able to live independently, in a dorm."

God. I'll be living without him. Something I've done for twenty-two years, granted, but not something that I imagined doing again.

I've never lived alone.

He is right about that. I've never had this experience, and it's one that I wanted.

"How will we…how will we see each other?"

"There are breaks. And I am a king. I have a private plane, and I'm allowed to fly in and out and—"

"*You* need to change that law," I say.

He puts his head against my shoulder. "Yes. I do."

"I'll go to school," I say, a deep lashing of grief hitting me. But this isn't the same grief as before. This is something different. This is something entirely unexpected. I'm getting what I want. He's not stopping me from it. Not anymore. So why do I feel so…sad? It's like when I found out I wasn't pregnant. Like when I found out he wanted me to go on the pill, which was a good thing, except…it means I'm not trapped with him. Maybe it even means that I'm not as important to him as I was.

CHAPTER TWELVE

The Dragon

THE PALACE IS quiet and something in me aches. I've never felt this before. I've known grief. I've known the impossibility of missing people you can never see again. This is something else.

Everything echoes. The halls, my chest.

I've forgotten how to be alone, after years of knowing nothing else.

CHAPTER THIRTEEN

MY ACCOMMODATION IS nothing standard for a university student. It's not on campus, but in a building nearby that offers more luxury, which I would never have asked for, but Lucian insists. I don't have a roommate and it's… Well, it's nothing like I thought. In that it isn't spare, and I'm certainly not scraping pennies together. Lucian made sure that I have the most up-to-date computer—I wasn't even sure how to use it at first because I have such an old one and I'm so used to letting everything lag for a while. There is no lag.

The room is fit for a princess—and I guess I'm a queen. That's a strange aspect to all of this. Alabria is a small enough country that I'm not so well known that I'm recognized at fifty paces, especially when I'm dressed down like any other college student—no makeup and I've taken to wearing glasses I don't need so that I look a bit more serious and a bit less like myself.

I'm not a campus celebrity—but I'm not anonymous either.

In the three weeks since I've started school I've had three private meltdowns, about four out-of-body experiences, two texts from Lucian and I've made four friends. They've been very polite about getting details on my personal life, but tonight we're having a girl dinner in my room—a smattering of cheeses, meats, bread and a lot of candy and wine—and all circumspection has ended.

"So, you're a queen," Tefi says, looking at me as somberly as she can after two glasses of wine.

"I suppose," I say, sounding as regretful as I can after my own two glasses of wine.

"But you're at university," Alexandra says.

"Yes, but at first my husband said—"

"Husband!!" Elektra and Zuri howl.

"I mean," Zuri says, looking apologetic, "I knew you had a husband but it's just so odd to hear you say it."

Yes, of course, because everyone else here is experimenting with dating and kissing and sex. I'm somewhere past *experimentation*. I've had what I'm sure is the best sex anyone could hope for.

I miss it. I miss him.

"Lucian de Mornay, King of Alabria. Age forty—lord girl, that's dodgy." Tefi is eyeballing her phone, with the stats she's just googled on my husband. "And you're his third wife. Blink if you need help." She's giggling but I wonder if she's half serious. "No, for real, were you trafficked?"

Yes, she is serious.

"No," I say. "He's paying for me to go to school. I'm not a prisoner or anything. And yes, he's older than me and he's got a past, but he…"

"Is it a love match or are you in a marriage of convenience?"

"Complicated," I mumble, grabbing a pillow and holding it to my chest.

"Ohh." Tefi looks wide-eyed now. "You love him."

"Well, I… He's great in bed." I say this to get a reaction out of them, and maybe even to sound experienced, which, in some ways I am, because Lucian is a creative lover even if he's been my only one.

"That's something anyway," Elektra says.

"Not a small something," Zuri says. "All the boys I've slept with here are shit."

Tefi laughs. "That's what you get with an older guy, I guess. Skill."

I snort. "Yeah, well, there is that. But also the added complication of the other wives."

"He doesn't still have them, does he?" Zuri asks.

"Did he murder them?" Tefi shrieks, still looking at her phone.

"No! And I want all that off the internet. He's just… He's a good man. He has some regrets about how he handled his past relationships—not murder regrets—but he's trying. I think he's trying to handle me differently." I'm trying to defend him without giving away his secrets.

"Well, now you're in another country," Elektra points out. "*You* can handle you however you want."

A couple of months ago I would have been very clear about what I wanted. I actually would have used this as a chance to escape. I would have gotten help from whoever I could and made sure I was able to stay here forever.

That's not what I want now.

My mom and sister are excited for me, but they can't understand why I'm living apart from my husband, and why I'm doing school when I could sit around being royalty.

I question that sometimes, though not for the same reasons they are.

As the term wears on I miss him and I'm miserable with it. I'm supposed to be having a wonderful time—and I am. I'm also stressed from all the work and questioning why I thought I could do this.

After a particularly heavy run of projects, I can breathe at least, but I haven't heard from Lucian.

"There's a party tonight down at the club, you should come." All my friends look at me expectantly and I balk.

"I can't just go to a nightclub!"

"No one will recognize you."

I have a security detail for when I leave the school, and I'm not sure what they'll think about me going off to a nightclub for a party. Though with some negotiation they agree to accompany me and my friends to the club.

I borrow a dress, which is much shorter than anything I normally wear, and we get party-ready, which is something I never did in my life before Lucian either. It is funny how my life feels so divided and defined by him and I'm reminded of what I said to him about virginity almost four months ago now. That a man doesn't have the power to change a woman with sex.

Maybe that's true. But with us it's never just been sex.

I feel beautiful, but I think that has to do with being in this group of friends. Who are complimenting me, and hyping me up, and for the first time in a while I feel like I'm not despairing. It's just been a really stressful stretch of time. Missing Lucian like I do, and having to do my coursework, I am feeling battered in a really strange way, and I'm not sure that I have the right to my feelings. Life has certainly been worse. But I can't say that I've ever been pulled in multiple directions this way.

And tonight feels like permission to indulge in something else. Something that has nothing to do with any aspect of my life.

My security detail gets us a limousine, which feels ridiculous, but it does fit our entire group, and get us to the club in relative style—the level of outrageousness is over the top. My friends are howling about how we actually look quite tacky, and I can't disagree.

But when we get into the club, I forget everything, because this is a whole new experience. Fun for the sake of it. I can't say that I've ever done that before. My whole life before Lucian was about earning my way here. Then everything with him has been…intense. I wouldn't call our relationship fun. It brings me to a place with myself that I've never been before. It's interesting; I can't deny that. And I miss it. I can't deny that either. But *fun* still isn't the word. Then there's this.

This long-held dream of mine finally happening. And I'm not sure that I could venture to call that fun either.

But this is. It's silly. And the drinks that we are getting are bright and fruity. The music is loud, and even though I've never danced in my life, I am getting into the swing of it. I'm dizzy, dancing with my friends and having a brilliant time of it. For the first time in my life I'm not unbearably conscious of who I am. Of everything that I feel like I'm holding up. I'm just having fun. And if part of me aches for Lucian, I do the best that I can to push that part of myself away. Because yes, certainly, it would be lovely if he could be here with me. If he could be the kind of man who could take me out and dance with me. Who could laugh with me.

I think about our days in my room, curled up on the floor with books. He does laugh sometimes. So that isn't really fair of me.

But he doesn't laugh easily, and the trouble is neither do I, so it's a whole difficult thing for us to draw it out of one another. Maybe I'll learn to laugh a little bit more freely during my time here. Maybe I'll be able to bring back that to our marriage.

To our life.

Our life. This is my life here. It isn't him and me. And maybe that's how he feels too. Maybe the palace is his life. God knows he's always treated it that way. Like it's his to control and command, and I'm just a piece of it.

I grit my teeth and pushed that thought to the side. I don't especially want it at the moment.

No. I'm trying to have fun. I don't need to think about Lucian at all.

A man approaches me on the dance floor, objectively handsome, I suppose. Close to my age, and I move rather deftly away. But he keeps following me wherever I weave to on the dance floor, until his hands go to my hips, and he looks me in the eye. "Are you deliberately trying to avoid me?"

I feel like I've been captured by a hunter. "Well, yes," I say.

He grins. "I don't mind a chase, but I do like to know if my quarry is interested."

He's leaning in very close, because the music is loud, and there is no other option.

"I'm married," I say.

He draws back, looking shocked. "That's not typical."

"No, I'm sure not. I'm sorry."

"Does that mean you weren't looking for a partner tonight?"

Suddenly, my body aches. With missing Lucian. His touch. His possession. I would love to have a partner tonight. But it would have to be him. The music just feels too loud now, and I'm too hot. And I don't want this man.

"No," I say. "Just my husband for me. But…thank you. It's flattering." I feel bad turning him down, maybe because I've never turned a man down in my life before. "I have friends," I say, gesturing to the group.

He looks quite interested in that.

"And believe me when I tell you, some of them are looking."

Which is how he ends up with the group for the majority of the evening, and it's Tefi who ends up winning his attentions, and I try not to feel nervous when she elects to leave with him. Though, I do end up sending a security detail to follow them. I figure it's a very normal thing for people to hook up with strangers, but I have every right to feel responsible for how this goes, given that I'm the one that allowed him to join the group. Which means I can send my security detail out with them.

We all leave the club bedraggled and tipsy at two in the morning, and I fall into bed and wake up when my phone buzzes ferociously. It's only six, and I feel vile. My head is pounding.

"Hello?"

It's Zuri.

"Oh God, girl. You're in trouble."

"Why?" I sit up, and I try to think around my pounding head, and my dry mouth.

"Your picture with that dude got put all over the internet. And people are acting like you were hooking up with him."

"What? But Tefi left with him."

"Yes. Careful editing on the part of the people who posted the photos. They just put up pictures of you talking with him and bringing him to the group. And of course you've been identified as the Queen of Alabria, out cheating on your old husband."

"I wouldn't… I… I would never."

"I know that, but it's all viral now and everything."

"God. Lucian is going to see this."

"Yeah. So I would do some damage control with him if I were you. I mean, everyone is cheering you on, and praising you for being out living your life, but then the other issue is it's now widespread knowledge that you're going to university."

People did know, but it didn't matter before. Because there was no narrative. I open up my phone and google myself, and find the story faster than I would like. The emancipation of the Queen of Alabria. Like I'm the prisoner. Except I was. And… Why is this so… complicated?

Because a lot of the things that they say about him are true. But they don't know him. And they don't understand. They're also diminishing me, the role that I played in our marriage. The way that I chose him. How much I want him. It's all turned into this thing about him manipulating me, taking advantage of the power differential, but of course says nothing about how I stepped in and chose to marry him instead of my sister. And of course they act like he installed me at university as a place to keep me, ignoring that I got myself in, and he wanted me to go because he…cared what I wanted.

It makes me hate everyone.

I try calling Lucian, but he doesn't answer his phone. So I spend the day texting him, and he doesn't respond to me. I'm worried, worried that my marriage is over. Worried that this breach is something that we are never going to be able to come back from. Doesn't he know me well enough to know that I would never cheat on him?

And anyway, I thought he didn't care about his reputation. But now suddenly my dragon is what? Pouting in his cave because people think that I cheated?

That's not fair. If he's upset about it, he certainly has a right to be. I'm not happy about story either, but I didn't do anything wrong. I didn't do anything wrong, and he's not communicating with me.

I call him five more times; he doesn't answer.

And I spend the next several days at school being a celebrity in a way that I've never wanted to be. Deeply regrettably, this has also opened me up to men thinking that I'm an easy target, and so I'm also fending off advances left and right, which I can certainly say has never happened to me before.

"I hear you're up for a good time," some random bloke says to me in a common area, and I finally lose it.

"I'm married! And I'm not sleeping with some random when I have a king with a castle back at home."

Where are my online stalkers when I have a tantrum like that in public? Certainly not posting anything that goes viral.

My friends tried to cheer me up through the entire thing. My mother and sister video call me with deep concern. And I tell them that nothing actually happened. But of course the one person I actually want to speak to does nothing to get in touch with me.

I sit alone in my room, feeling… I don't even know what. Is it heartbreak? Can it possibly be when no declarations of feelings have been shared by anyone? I'm deeply wounded by the entire thing. But most of all, by Lucian's silence.

This is just like every man every woman in my family has lo—

Oh, it hurts.

I care for him so much more than I wanted to. I didn't protect myself, and now I'm broken.

It feels like a betrayal. It feels like a real lack of trust in me. That he would let us be broken over this.

I start to worry about him so much that my grades suffer. Which infuriates me. Because being here isn't supposed to be about him. It's supposed to be about me. He isn't speaking to me, so why can't I just not think of him? I'm living my dream, and I'm worried about this man that's only been in my life for a few months. To the point that he's all I can think about. To the point that his silence feels more imposing than his presence ever has.

And it feels like another thing he's forced upon me. And I am over it.

Which is why, at the end of term, after my final exams, when I see a large silhouette standing in front of my room, I am confused. My heart leaps up into my throat, and I feel certain that it can only be one person. But that one person hasn't even returned a single text of mine, so how can he be here in person?

Why would he be?

It doesn't even seem possible. I'm hallucinating. That's how badly I want to see him.

"Lucian?"

He turns, and everything inside of me combusts. He's here. He came to see me. He came—

His expression looks grave. What if he's here to end our marriage?

I'm not going to let them do that. I'm not going to let them say that. I fling myself across the space, and throw my arms around him. "You came for me."

Slowly, he wraps his arms around my waist. "You're happy to see me?"

I pull away from him. "You idiot. I've been calling you. Texting you. Trying to make sure that you're not angry with me."

"I'm not angry with you. I wanted to give you space."

"Space? I didn't ask you for space. When a person calls you and texts you, generally they're asking for connection."

"I thought perhaps you needed a chance to explore certain things."

"Lucian. Do you mean…? Did you think that I hooked up with that man?"

"No," he says, his voice raw grit, like it's being pulled through his teeth. "I didn't. I didn't because I know how wrong the press gets it all the time. But it did make me think that perhaps you were wanting the chance to do something else. The article did have a point. I am older than you and—"

"I have no interest in boys. I have no interest in anyone who isn't you."

"Perhaps you only *think* that."

"No. I was a twenty-two-year-old virgin not because

I could've never found a man to take my virginity, but because I never found one who interested me. You know, men are notoriously not particular about who they sleep with."

"You are gorgeous," he says. "You can have any man you desire. I'm not trying to say that you couldn't. But I am saying that things are different here, and you have more opportunity."

"I don't *want* the opportunity. Next time, pick up the phone. Don't make decisions for me."

He looks raw, and angry. He looks desperate. His shoulders sag, and for the first time, I see Lucian defeated. "I stayed away as long as I could. I couldn't manage it anymore."

"Thank God."

Then he kisses me, roughly. And I open up the door to my apartment, closing it and locking it behind us. I think of all the times, all the ways in which he has reduced me to a creature filled with nothing more than want and need. And I want the same for him. I don't want him to have control.

Because that's the real problem with the way all of this played out. He had the control. He was the one who chose not to contact me. As much as he saw that as giving me something, it speaks to his ability to stay away from me when I can't stay away from him. I want him to feel the way that I do. I want him to feel desperate, reduced. I don't want him to have all this power. The media's wrong about where the power lies.

It's not in him being older. It's not in him being a king. It's in his ability to withhold himself.

I think of all the times he's given me three orgasms to his one. All the times that he's turned our intimacy into my own sexual torture.

It's wonderful, glorious. And yet at the same time, he is the master of it.

I want to be the master. I want to be the one in charge of everything we are.

Of all this heat and glory.

I want him naked, in front of me while I remain fully clothed.

"Sit down," I say. It's an order, and I'm not certain that King Lucian has ever obeyed an order in his life. But he does so, pours his large frame into the wing-back chair that sits by the fireplace. "Take your clothes off," I say.

"You are in no position—"

"Yes, I am," I say. "I am the queen. And I demand that you make amends for the way that you've treated me. I feel extremely ill used. And I want to see my husband naked. Because of course I haven't slept with anyone else. Haven't kissed them, haven't touched them. Have you, my king?"

"Of course not," he growls.

"Then you must be as desperate as I am."

"I need you," he says, and for the first time I see a spark of frayed control.

"If you're desperate, then show me. Take your clothes off."

He begins to obey, slowly, his scarred hands working to undo the buttons on his shirt. He strips his shirt away, throws it down onto the floor. Then he undoes his belt, lifts his hips up off the chair and strips his trousers and underwear down. He's naked, and extremely aroused, his cock standing proud and tempting against his flat stomach. How strange it is that I've lived all this time without him. All this time without sex. And yet, now I feel desperate. Now I feel like living without it is killing me.

Perhaps it is just him. Perhaps it's only everything we are.

I move to him, and I kiss him. I settle myself on his lap, loop my arms around his neck, kiss his mouth, his neck, and then I move to his body, exploring that broad, scarred chest. I slide down to the floor, kissing his stomach, his thigh, working my way to his cock.

He grips my hair as my mouth hovers over him. "I don't have control."

"I don't want you to have control," I say.

I lean in then I flick my tongue over the broad head of him. I've missed this. The taste of him, the feel of him. I've missed him more than I can possibly say. My whole body aches with it. It's like I'm complete again for the first time. It's like I can breathe again.

This has been wonderful. It's been my dream. But it's a dream dimmed, because I'm not complete when I'm not with Lucian. That's just a burden that I have to bear. The truth that I have to reckon with.

But not now. Now I'm simply going to luxuriate in him. In our mutual desire. And how much he needs me. Just as much as I need him. I'm proving it. I swallow him down as deep as I can take him, showing him my devotion. Showing him just how much I want him.

Just how much I crave him. I tighten my hand around his thick base as I take in as much as I possibly can. I pull away for a moment, and he grips my chin, tilting my face up so that we make eye contact.

"They'll wish they could have you," he says, rubbing his thumb over my lower lip. "Because look at what a goddess you are. None of these boys are worthy of getting this from you."

I shake my head. "And I would never, ever give it to them."

"Mine. That mouth is mine."

I nod. "Only yours." Then I lean in, and I take him and again, I lose myself in this. In the desire that's burning between us, powered by something deeper than simple physical need.

He tries to pull my head away as he begins to lose his control. He doesn't like to finish this way. He always wants to be inside of me, and I know that. But I'm not going to let him. I'm not going to give him what he wants. I'm going to give myself what I want. I'm going to indulge in this man, who I've missed more than words can say.

I'm going to have what's mine.

Then he arches up, hitting the back of my throat, emptying himself, and I swallow him down, the flavor of him the most glorious thing I've ever had.

I rest my head on his thigh, and he strokes my hair. I smile, feeling wicked. "I think I've decided what my very favorite meal is," I say.

He makes a short, masculine sound in the back of his throat. "Sparrow..."

"It's you. So, you can stop asking me now."

I kiss the top of his thigh, and he grips my hair and tilts my face up so that I'm looking at him. "You are reckless, and dangerous."

"Because of you," I say.

He lifts me up from the floor and bundles me onto his lap, stroking my hair.

"Did you really miss me?"

His words are almost soft. They make my throat ache.

"Yes," I say. "It's actually quite miserable. Here I am in this place that I've always wanted to be. This place that I've always wanted to live. And I can't stop thinking about you."

I stand up, still completely clothed, while he's entirely naked. I move around the room, humming happily to myself.

"I think we shall stay here during your term break," he says.

"Here?"

"In England. There's no need for us to return to the palace. We can do more sightseeing. Whatever it is you want."

"I don't really care," I say. "I want to be with you."

"Do you want to go to nightclubs? Do you want… to spend time with your friends? You do have friends. You mentioned that in your texts."

"Oh, you read my texts."

"Yes, dammit. I read your texts. I'm… Is that what you would like?"

I shake my head. "No. I'll see my friends during the

term. What I would like is to spend time with you. I was afraid that wasn't going to happen."

"Well, maybe we should change what that time looks like."

I touch his chest, and look at him in the eye. "I would like to not leave our bed."

I am resolute in this. I'm a little bit surprised. Or at least, some distant version of myself is surprised. Why don't I want to take this opportunity to travel the world? To see more things? Things that I've always dreamed of.

I'm being given this extraordinary, exquisite opportunity, and I am not taking it. I don't know what that is. Except that it just feels like the whole world will always be there, and Lucian is what I want. Living, breathing. Everything.

"I would like to meet your friends," he says.

"All right," I say. "I think everyone is still here. I can see if they'd like to have dinner?"

"Yes. I will take everyone out to dinner."

I'm somewhat amused at the very idea of this, but Lucian, this reclusive, strange creature that he is, is offering to have a dinner that has nothing to do with diplomacy, or anything really but me. And I want to take him up on it.

Of course, he has to arrange private dining; he is a king.

My group text is a flurry of activity, and everyone is thrilled to meet my husband, but also slightly terrified of him.

I've told them, repeatedly, that he's not actually

scary. But the truth is, his mere presence is intimidating, whether or not I feel it still. So, I can't really blame them for feeling as if there's something intimidating about him.

I'm used to Lucian. Sort of. *Used to* is a really difficult descriptor for a man like him. But I suppose I'm used to him in context. In his castle, in a diplomatic setting, where his presence feels larger-than-life, and the setting around him is as well.

But in this restaurant, at a table with myself, and my friends, he seems almost laughably out of place. Like a relic brought forward in time and placed somewhere that he absolutely doesn't belong.

Everything looks a bit too small for him. And a bit too civilized.

It takes a good while for anyone to find traction with conversation, and I feel an immense amount of pressure, because it seems like I should be able to build a bridge between Lucian and my friends, considering that I know them both, but I'm not even sure what bridge the both of them could walk over.

A strange way of looking at it, but I find that I can't help it.

"And Elektra is majoring in infectious disease with a focus on sexually transmitted diseases," I say, having just gone through the litany of things that my friends are studying.

"Fascinating," Lucian says.

"Thank you," Elektra says. "And you're…a king."

"Yes," Lucian says.

"What's that like?" Tefi asks.

"I'm not really sure," he says. "Only because I don't really know what it's like to not be one."

"Well, that's fair," says Zuri. "I dated a rugby player who was also the son of a man who was knighted. So, kind of close."

"Kind of," Lucian says.

"Have you streamed any good TV shows recently?" Zuri asks.

Everyone looks at her.

"What? I think it's interesting to know what a king watches."

"I read," he says. "Mostly."

"Oh yes," I say. "Lucian loves fiction."

"Oh, me too," says Elektra. "Mostly smut, though."

"I'm not opposed," Lucian says.

"Maybe we can trade book recommendations," Elektra says.

That is maybe the least painful part of the evening. And it's fine. It's just… Lucian isn't a twentysomething college student. He's a king. He moves like a king; he acts like a king. He isn't going to mesh with this life. And that's just one of the many difficult things about the moment that I have to contend with.

My life has two pieces to it that are somewhat incompatible. It creates tension inside of me. But this is what I've always wanted to do. I've always wanted to have a university experience, and I'm having it. But this particular university experience requires me to be away from him. And when he's with me here it's… it's a little bit of a thing. But it was lovely of him to have dinner with me and my friends. It was extremely sweet that he wanted to try. Maybe we'll do this sometimes, maybe it will get less awkward or maybe it never will, because…because Lucian was never one who had friends, so even if age and experience and him being a king didn't separate him from that group, the fact that he wasn't able to make friends as a boy probably would.

When we get back to my room, I laugh and throw myself onto the bed.

"What?" he asks.

"Oh, it was very awkward," I say.

"Was it?"

He looks very concerned.

"It's okay. Lucian, you're a king. Small talk is probably never going to be part of your repertoire. And that's okay. I don't want to make small talk with you anyway."

He moves to the bed, and kisses me. "Good. Because I don't want to talk right now either."

CHAPTER FOURTEEN

By the end of the term break, I miss my friends, and I feel grumpy because I'm going to be separated from Lucian again. I actually miss Alabria more than I ever thought possible. For all that I felt stuck there for most of my life, it's my home. And being the queen has made me feel that in a more profound way than I could've possibly imagined.

I'm also missing my mother, my sister. This is the longest I've ever gone without seeing them in person. I feel like I'm being pulled in ten different directions. Lucian seems to have noticed my low mood, because dinner is the most extravagant affair we've had since coming to the country house. There's a table set out on the lawn, candles illuminating everything. The table has a silk, dusky purple covering, the plates made of gold. Thc food is exquisite, French and finely executed. Because for all that he is my favorite meal, I do still enjoy food of a more traditional variety.

He has arranged for me to have a brand-new dress for dinner, and the copper color suits me. When I looked at my reflection, I was so pleased with what I saw.

It was an interesting moment. One that allowed me to reflect on everything that's changed. I'm not the same person that I was all that time ago. All that short time ago. I'm not, and could never be. It used to be that all I cared about was staying safe. Emotionally. I told myself that it was because I wanted to learn. Because I wanted to make it to university. But the truth is, I've been running from this part of myself for a very long time. The one that wants good food. The one that wants to feel pretty. The one that wants to feel cherished by a romantic partner. And I do.

I…

Everything about him is beyond a dream. Because he's a dream I wouldn't let myself have.

I had no expectations of him. Of us. And it's far beyond anything I could've ever hoped for.

I understand, though, why I didn't want it. Even if it were possible. Because it isn't so simple as being happy because you've found someone to care for.

It means that I'm in a constant state of tension with myself. Because when I'm away from him I have to miss him. And in order to accomplish some of the other things that I want to accomplish, I have to miss him.

"Tell me everything about what's happening in Alabria," I say.

"Well, since ending my embargo on flights, an entirely new industry is opening up, and I'm busy funding airlines and routes to the island. Now there has to be an airport expansion."

"Oh," I say. "So that's an entire can of worms."

"Yes. A good one. One that's already stimulating the

economy. And for that, I have you to thank. You're the one that pushed me to do that."

"I think you would've gotten there yourself," I say. "Eventually."

"Perhaps. Eventually. But it certainly wasn't a conclusion I was arriving at easily."

"That's okay," I say. "Sometimes it takes a minute. To figure out change. I mean, that's been basically my whole existence for the past few months."

"Yes," he says, looking at me gravely. "It has been."

"Not a bad thing. To have to change. I was afraid of so many things when we first met, Lucian. And it isn't even something I was aware of. I was afraid of feeling too much."

"And now?" he asks.

"Oh, I still think it's quite terrible. But… I'm not scared of it anymore."

It's been so lovely, being with him here in the country house. It's the closest thing to being back home with him in the palace. Reading together, talking, eating, making love. Those are the beautiful aspects of who we are. Who we really are. There are other things that we do. He runs an entire country. I'm going to school. But these are the things that we choose to do when we have nothing and no one else to please. And that is its own wonderful discovery.

After dinner, he takes me up to bed. And there's something driving me tonight that's different than any other night. It's our last one together for a while. I'm just so much sadder about it than I thought that I would be. Than I imagined I could be. I kiss him, deep and desperate. I pour everything into that kiss. Everything that I don't want to name. Everything that I've been holding back.

Because the truth is, I've been holding something back for a while. From him, from myself. A revelation that I wasn't quite ready for. A realization that I didn't want to fully embrace. Because it means that I…that I've given in. That I've surrendered. To this forced marriage, to this need between us, to this change. This true, fundamental change in what I want.

But I don't actually think it's a change in who I am.

No. This is who I've always wanted to be. Secretly, deep down. What I want to do, where I want to live, that isn't who I am. But this, passionate, sensual, adventurous, brave and open, this is what I've always wanted. But what I've always feared.

So I embrace it now, as I kiss him. As I strip his clothes off, and mine. As I kiss my way down his body, and let my need guide us.

He's content with that for a while, but then, something changes in his face. He becomes like a man possessed, kissing me, lifting me up and pressing me against the wall, our naked bodies entwined, his fingers pushed through my hair.

Often, he's reverent with me. Tonight, he's rough. He kisses me, licks into me like a starving man, then moves his hands over my curves, down my hips, presses his hand between my legs as he begins to stroke me, driving me higher and higher, pushing me to the edge. He drops to his knees before me, roughly parting my legs and worshipping me, as he did that first time we were together. As he's done many times since, but this is different than all of them. There's an edge. One that I can't define, but one that I'm captive to all the same.

I scream as I tumble over into oblivion, and I don't care if someone hears. I don't care about anything. Not anything but this thing between us.

That night that I went out to the nightclub, I was euphoric because I had nothing to worry about. Nothing to overthink about.

I thought, for a moment, that it was something I wanted more of. I don't. I want more of this. This weighty, difficult glory.

This is the most real thing in my life. The most important thing that I could ever have. I could study out of different textbooks, I could build different connections, make different friends. I could go to any number of universities, and there would be something wonderful to be gleaned from each of them. It doesn't mean that this university, that my friends aren't important, but I can see a life where I move through different phases. Where those things wax and wane like the moon and the tide. Where they become more and less essential parts of who I am.

Lucian isn't like that.

He's essential. My foundation. The thing that I need. Lucian is like breathing.

The difference between Lucian and everything else is that I'm in love with him.

That deep, sweeping love that my mother, my sister, have spent all their lives looking for. They fling themselves into the passion, and hope that it becomes this. And I've got it.

The glory and the terror of it.

There will never be another man. Not like him.

There will never be another passion; there will never be another love. Not like this one.

He is not a phase; he's not a rising tide. He is the mountain upon which all other things are built.

The rock upon which everything I am stands.

And no wonder I didn't want to admit it. Because it's so big, so frightening, but it's also deeply satisfying, soothing in a way.

To know that I found this.

This thing that I wanted to avoid. Because of course it cracks you open and makes you vulnerable. Because it makes you hurt, because it makes you bleed. Because it makes what he wants just as important as what I want. Because it means that if I'm away from him, I will always be a little bit sad.

He lifts me up, and lays me down on the bed, and I give thanks that I'm on the pill, so we can be together without a barrier, which I had missed. Because I love the feel of him. I love the hot spill of him inside of me, because I love to claim as much of him as possible.

And when he thrusts deep, it feels like I'm complete. Like I don't know where he begins and I end, and I don't want to. I have been fiercely independent, and desperately avoidant of anything like this for all of my life.

And now I have embraced it. Quite literally. I wrap my arms around him, and I kiss his face, kiss his mouth, as he thrusts into me, as his movements become rough and unmeasured. As we melt into each other. As we both lose control.

He comes apart, and so do I, and I hold him, as tight as I can.

"It's so difficult to say goodbye," I say.

"But…you love school," he says.

"Yes," I say, my heart soaring with the revelation of a few moments ago. "But, Lucian, I love you."

His face turns to stone, and I see fire in his eyes. I know he doesn't know what to do with this. I know it's been so long since anyone has said it to him that he doesn't know what to make of it. I know him. His inability to say it back isn't a surprise. And it doesn't hurt my feelings. I understand him. I do.

"Then what does that mean?" he asks.

"That as long as I'm at school, as long as I'm away from you, even though it's my dream, I'm going to be a bit sad." I kiss his cheek. And lay my head on his chest.

I think there's something beautiful about this. Loving him so much that I hurt with it. That I carry it with me as a painful badge of honor.

It's not what I planned for my life.

But as complicated as it is, I have never been happier. Even as I carry the sadness.

Because this is what it means to really live. To be whole. And I take a certain measure of joy in that, even as I begin to weep.

CHAPTER FIFTEEN

The Dragon

I HAVE CURSED my sparrow to a life of sadness. If she had never known me, then she would never know this pain. I can see clearly where I've gone wrong. I know she thinks she loves me. But Stockholm syndrome is a very real thing, and I fear that I may have inflicted it on her. Never have I been more conscious of how much younger she is than when I went to dinner with her friends. I had nothing to say to any of them. She wanted so badly to bring me into that part of her life, and I will never be able to inhabit it. Even if I weren't older, I'm scarred. It's been too many years of isolation. It's been too much time of me curating that isolation. I've let everyone believe that I'm hard-hearted, to the extent that I began to believe it too.

Only Lilith has ever made me feel differently. She is the only one that has ever made me want to find something softer inside myself.

And I know that I have no choice now. I started this. I have to end it.

I know she doesn't want me making choices for her, but this all began with a choice I made for her. This all began with me forcing her into my life.

With me clipping her wings. I tried to remove the cage. But I can see now that unless I remove myself I can never truly undo the damage that I've done.

So I will do what I have to, to let her truly fly.

CHAPTER SIXTEEN

THE START OF a new term, new classes, does bring a certain measure of excitement with it. But God I miss him.

"He is very sexy," Tefi says, as I brood over lunch.

"Yes," I say. "I just… I'm so in love with him it's painful, and it would be a lot more convenient if we'd been married for longer before I did this. But of course it made more sense for me to do it before we had kids."

"It's just so funny to me," Tefi says, "that you're there. I mean, that you have a man that you're this sick in love with, and you're ready to have his kids. Most of us are just able to focus on the education bit."

I laugh. "That was my plan. But…it's all right. It's not how it worked out."

I really do mean that. Because I get why my friends find this to be strange and alien. But I watched Tefi moon over that guy who hooked up with her, then ghosted her, then slid back into her DM's, hooked up with her relentlessly over the term, then vanished again. I've watched Zuri go through a disastrous series of dates, with each guy being more disappointing than the last, and then finally, poor Elektra getting love bombed by the girl she just started seeing, who wanted to move into the same room at school almost instantaneously, only to blow it all up three weeks later.

There is no existing without drama, not in this life. Mine feels like a settled sort of drama anyway.

I go back to my room at the end of the day, and frown when I see an envelope on my pillow. It's a fancy one, sealed with Lucian's seal.

I open it up, and pull out a handwritten letter.

Sparrow,

I realize that what I've done to you is wrong. I keep trying to make something that I forced on you into your choice, but I can never truly do that if I don't let you go. Our marriage is over. I've dissolved it here in Alabria. I don't want to hurt you. But I fear that I must free you decisively. Or you will always be a little bit sad.

I cannot bear that I've done this to you. I want to give you your life back. Utterly and completely. The rest of your time at school is paid for. All of your expenses. There is money in an account for you, and you will never want for anything, ever again, neither will your mother and sister. This is all I know how to do to fix this. I have never cared if the world thought that I was a monster. But I cannot be a monster to you.

I know what they call me. And they say a dragon craves a virgin sacrifice. I do not want you to be a sacrifice to me. Please, go. Be free of me.

Lucian

My hands begin to shake, and then my whole body. He's doing it again. Making decisions for me. And I understand how it's twisted in his head. He feels like I've been manipulated into all of this. He feels like none of the choices have been mine. But he's wrong. I love him. I choose him. I have to figure out some way to convince him of that. I'm furious. Because how dare he? How dare he decide that he knows what's best? But of course he has. But this letter… What I need to know is if this means he loves me. If it means he loves me, or if he is still atoning for Colette. If he's still atoning for feeling like he's responsible for the death of his parents. I need to know. And I'll only be able to know if I go to him.

Thank God there are commercial flights into Alabria now.

Because I am going to surprise him where he is. I'm going to have to miss classes.

But this is more important.

I know for sure, this is more important.

When I land in Alabria, I go straight to the palace. I've warned my security detail not to pass any information on to Lucian, and after explaining the situation, they actually did listen to me. They see the same thing I do. That Lucian is a good man, trapped in his own grief. He's pushing me away; I know it. I feel that he believes this is the right thing. What I really need to know is why.

I walk into the palace, and it reminds me of that first

day that I ever met him. When he sat on that throne and gazed at me with his indolent, golden stare.

But now, I know him. Now, I love him. Now, I'm not afraid.

I'm not here for my sister anymore. I'm here for me. And nothing has ever felt more powerful.

I storm past the guards, and into the throne room. "King Lucian," I say. "I do not accept your divorce. I love you. And I need to know if you love me."

CHAPTER SEVENTEEN

The Dragon

Five months ago

I've been informed by my guards that I'm to expect a replacement wife. But I have no idea who this creature is. Lilith. Such a funny name, in contrast to her sister, Eve. I wonder if her mother did it on purpose. Eve is beautiful; I've seen photographs of her. We've done all the intel necessary to decide whether or not she will be a good fit for me. Perversely, she reminds me of Emerald, who ran away from me, and I take some delight in that, mainly because I know it will unsettle Emerald herself. I don't care. She's off married to her bodyguard now, and that's fine with me.

But if I can't play mind games with people, what is life?

My reputation for being a bastard is well documented, and I'm rather fond of it.

It keeps people away. I sit there, and I wait.

The doors open, and there she is.

It is the strangest sensation I've ever known. It's as if the heavens quieted for a moment, and then opened up, light pouring down upon her. It's like I can see clearly for the first time in my life, and it's also like everything has suddenly fallen to pieces. Like it is destroyed and remade all in one breath. All because of her.

Her hair is a golden blonde, her eyes almost green. There is a mysterious quality about her. As if she is herself a secret garden that can only truly be known and explored by one willing to look.

I have read so many stories. About love, about adventure, about hope. All these things have evaded me, and it's like in one sweeping moment she brought it all into the room with her. I cannot explain it, but it's like this one woman contains inside her every beautiful work of fiction I've ever known, made flesh, standing there in front of me.

And I know, immediately and with no hesitation, that I will do anything for her.

I need to keep her.

I need to make sure that she never leaves me. That she's never at risk. That nothing ever happens to her. I need this woman to continue to breathe. I thought, many years ago, that I loved my wife. Because she was pretty, and I enjoyed her body. Because I felt grief when she died. But I've never known anything like this. This is love. Something bigger than me.

Something bigger than all the forces in the universe. Beyond explanation, beyond reason.

And the beast inside of me roars with conviction.

I will keep her. I will cage her. I will make her mine. So that she will never want anything or anything else ever again.

CHAPTER EIGHTEEN

The Dragon

Now

SHE'S HERE. And it's like I can breathe for the first time in days. She shouldn't be here. I ended this for a reason. I ended it for her own good. That she doesn't seem to recognize this angers me. But she doesn't know how vile I am. She doesn't know how all I've wanted from the moment I met her was to trap her. She doesn't know the depths of my obsession.

I wanted to add her to the stores of treasure in the palace, and I was willing to shrink her, to reshape her into my image of the queen I wanted, to keep her.

I *thought* that I fell in love with her the first moment that I saw her. But I never really knew what love was until I was willing to let her go.

There is a saying, and I've read it before, but nothing made it feel real. If you love something, let it go. If it's meant to be it will find its way back.

But she's just stubborn. She's stubborn, and she's not allowing me to make the right decision for her.

Enraging girl.

"What are you doing here?"

"I'm here for you, you idiot. You've done it again. You made choices for us without talking to me."

"Because I had to," I say. "Lilith, don't you understand, if it wasn't for me, you would be off living your life, with no regrets, and no sorrow whatsoever. I had to do what needed to be done to give that back to you."

"You cannot make me fall out of love with you any more than you can take the sun out of the sky."

"I will take the sun out of the sky. I'll figure it out. I'll do whatever I need to do."

"Why?"

"Because I—"

"Why?" she says, moving nearer to me. "Is it because you feel guilty about what happened with Colette?"

"*Yes*," I say, because I know that's the right answer to give to make her leave.

This whole thing has been a study in living contradictions, in being torn apart. I've wanted to draw her close and push her away by turns so many times over these past months.

She has bewitched me, body and soul.

She is my secret garden.

She is my sparrow.

She looks at me, and I know she doesn't believe me. "Why?" she asks again.

"You foolish girl. You deserve better than this. More

than this. You deserve to live your life on your own terms. You certainly don't deserve to be trapped with a man who doesn't understand the first thing about love. You have all this time left ahead of you, and you deserve to live unencumbered."

"Do I deserve to live without the love of my life?"

"You deserve a different love."

"I don't want it," she says.

"You don't know what you want."

"You said once that I was very smart. Clever. Do you not believe that anymore?"

"Of course I do. But you are good with science—that doesn't mean that you understand this. It doesn't mean that this is the right thing."

"I deserve to be part of the decision-making. You cannot save everyone. Even Colette, she made her choice, Lucian, and you have to accept it. Your parents made their choice, you have to accept it. You do not hold the world together, and you do not hold people to you, or apart from you. You did it. You gave me freedom, you gave me the means to live without you. And I'm choosing to live with you."

"You need to go to school."

"I need to know that I have you. And whatever else I choose to do on top of that, that's just the way that I choose to live life. It's different than choosing who I share my life with. It's different than choosing that fundamental piece of who I am. I love you. That is essential to me. Nonnegotiable to me. I'm your wife. I'm the Queen of Alabria. You are my new dream. And I deserve the respect that I know myself well enough to know what I'm choosing."

"But it cannot possibly be me."

I am broken. I am cold and difficult, I have never known connection to another person until her. And it feels too good to be true that I might have found it now.

That one day, my dream walked into my throne room, broke into my isolation.

That she found me.

How can this be?

It is beyond miraculous and it seems a foolish thing to believe—a fairy-tale thing.

She takes a step toward me, and another. Until she has closed all the distance between us. Until she stops and puts her hand on my face. "Lucian, do you remember what I told you about my dreams? About the way that I was too afraid to have them? I think you're afraid. And I believe, I do believe that you want to do what's best for me, but I believe that you are truly scared of you being my choice because it means you need to hope. It means you need to love. And do it in a way that doesn't allow you to have absolute control."

"But…"

And I break apart. Because I realize what she's saying is true. Because I fell in love with her from the moment she walked in. And everything that I've tried to do since then has been about maintaining a level of control while allowing myself to have her, and when I realized that I couldn't do it anymore, I let her go completely. And all of this has been about keeping myself safe. All of this has been about running from the pain in my life.

I have known loss. Endless, horrible loss. I've known the cruelty of humanity and so rarely have I known the joy in it.

The feelings I have for her are so intense I wanted to protect myself in any way I could.

But I don't want to be safe.

I want her.

To be the hero of the story, you have to risk.

I will risk it all for her.

To be her hero.

"I love you," I say. "It isn't like anyone else. This isn't about guilt. You're right. It's about my fear. And I despise my own fear. Because when I was a boy and they were torturing me, I felt too much of it. I tasted too much of it. And now that I have the possibility of this happiness I find..." I stand up, and I kneel before her. "I fell in love with you the moment you walked into this throne room."

And with those words, I'm free.

As if they're a magical spell that lifted a curse from me. One I've been living under for far too long.

"What?"

"It's true," I say. "I loved you from the first moment that I saw you. You are everything I never allowed myself to want."

"That's what you are for me, Lucian. You are absolutely everything to me. I had the epiphany that I could want any number of other things for a career, for a focus of study, but I could never want another person the way that I want you."

"I have never had the option of choosing what I want to do with my life. But when you walked in it became clear. I want to love you. You are the fulfillment of every dream that I've ever had, of every story that I've ever read. I always wanted to escape my life. I wanted to read about people who weren't me. I wanted to connect, and sometimes fictional people were the only way to do that. Until you. You, and your resistance to reading good books. You, somehow, were instantly and immediately this missing piece to myself. Maybe because you are a scientist and I'm the furthest thing from it. Maybe because you're the first person to look at me and not be afraid of me."

"I'm more than not afraid of you," she says. "I love you."

I cannot remember the last time I heard the words, and she's said them to me so many times. A gift beyond anything that I've ever known.

"I love you," I say, holding her precious face. "I love you. I love you."

I realize that I've looked at everything the wrong way. It's been about what I allow. What I can bear. About what cage I put her in or release her from. All about changing her to suit me. When maybe we need to change together.

"The cage is open, sparrow," I say. "Let's fly together."

EPILOGUE

I FINISH STUDYING in a hybrid manner. I can't bear to be away from Lucian as often as school demands of me. But we work out ways for me to complete research in person, while I do the majority of my classes at the palace, which also allows me to sink into my duty as queen. After my graduation, we decide to have our first child.

A little boy. Beautiful, like his father. And I know that it will heal something in Lucian every day that he gets to be a father to him. Every day that he gets to keep him safe and unharmed. Every day that we get to build love as a family. He is a king, yes, but he pours lots of his time and energy into his family. As much as possible. He travels with me as I write papers, give speeches on my focus of research. Because I'm not doing it for him. I'm doing it for me. For the future that my children will be living in. I do it because I like it. And that's one of the greatest things of all.

That Lucian and I are living a life that we like. That we would choose, time and time again.

I'm even thankful now that he dissolved our marriage. Because after that, I had to choose to marry him all over again. And it was a very different wedding. Attended by my sister and her husband, my mother, and her newest boyfriend, who she's no longer with. With a dress that I chose for myself, with my best friends as bridesmaids and with only joy, and no fear at all.

For most of my life, I knew that I wanted to do one thing. With Lucian, I get to be a wife, a mother, a scientist, a queen.

But most of all, I'm his. And that is something I would choose every day, all over again, forever.

And every night, with our children, we read stories.

One in particular that might have been written by a certain king and released under a different name.

The Sparrow and the Dragon, about the impossible love between two creatures, from two different worlds.

It has a happy ending.

* * * * *

If you just couldn't get enough of
King's Captive Bride,
then be sure to check out the previous instalment in the Young, Hot and Royal trilogy,
Princess, Pregnant, Prisoner!

And why not explore these other stories by Millie Adams?

After-Hours Heir
Dragos's Broken Vows
Promoted to Boss's Wife
Heir of Scandal
From Convent to Queen

Available now!

Get up to 4 Free Books!

We'll send you 2 free books from each series you try PLUS a free Mystery Gift.

Both the **Harlequin Presents** and **Harlequin Medical Romance** series feature exciting stories of passion and drama.

YES! Please send me 2 FREE novels from Harlequin Presents or Harlequin Medical Romance and my FREE gift (gift is worth about $10 retail). I may cancel anytime by emailing ReaderServiceInfo@Harlequin.com or by calling 1-800-873-8635.If I don't cancel, I will receive 6 brand-new larger-print novels every month and be billed just $7.19 each in the U.S., or $7.99 each in Canada, or 4 brand-new Harlequin Medical Romance Larger-Print books every month and be billed just $7.19 each in the U.S. or $7.99 each in Canada. That's a savings of 20% off the cover price! It's quite a bargain! Shipping and handling is just 75¢ per book in the U.S. and $1.75 per book in Canada.* I understand that accepting the free books and gift places me under no obligation to buy anything—they are mine to keep for free no matter what I decide.

Choose one: ☐ **Harlequin Presents Larger-Print** (176/376 BPA G3CD) ☐ **Harlequin Medical Romance** (171/371 BPA G3CD) ☐ **Or Try Both!** (176/376 & 171/371 BPA G3CE)

Name (please print)

Address Apt. #

City State/Province Zip/Postal Code

Email: Please check this box ☐ if you would like to receive newsletters and promotional emails from Harlequin Enterprises ULC and its affiliates. You can unsubscribe anytime.

Mail to the **Harlequin Reader Service:**
IN U.S.A.: P.O. Box 1341, Buffalo, NY 14240-8531
IN CANADA: P.O. Box 603, Fort Erie, Ontario L2A 5X3

Want to explore our other series or interested in ebooks? Visit www.ReaderService.com or call 1-800-873-8635.

*Terms and prices subject to change without notice. Prices do not include sales taxes, which will be charged (if applicable) based on your state or country of residence. Canadian residents will be charged applicable taxes. Offer not valid in Quebec. This offer is limited to one order per household. Books received may not be as shown. Not valid for current subscribers to the Harlequin Presents or Harlequin Medical Romance series. All orders subject to approval. Credit or debit balances in a customer's account(s) may be offset by any other outstanding balance owed by or to the customer. Please allow 4 to 6 weeks for delivery. Offer available while quantities last.

Your Privacy — Your information is being collected by Harlequin Enterprises ULC, operating as Harlequin Reader Service. For a complete summary of the information we collect, how we use this information and to whom it is disclosed, please visit our privacy notice located at https://corporate.harlequin.com/privacy-notice. Notice to California Residents—Under California law, you have specific rights to control and access your data. For more information on these rights and how to exercise them, visit https://corporate.harlequin.com/california-privacy. For additional information for residents of other U.S. states that provide their residents with certain rights with respect to personal data, visit https://corporate.harlequin.com/other-state-residents-privacy-rights.

HPHM2603